Not with the Church's Money

a novella

By Michelle Stimpson & CaSandra McLaughlin

DISCARDED FROM THE
NASHVILLE PUBLIC LIBRARY

D0109657

Copyright © 2016 by CaSandra McLaughlin and Michelle Stimpson. All rights reserved. No part of this book may be reproduced in any form, except for brief quotations in reviews, without written permission from the author.

Published by Read for Joy, an imprint of MLStimpson Enterprises

The characters in this book are fictional. Any resemblance to actual people or events is coincidental.

Editing by Michelle Chester, www.ebm-services.com

Dedications

From CaSandra
For my brother Tyran Franklin.
I love you and I'm so proud of the man you've become.

From Michelle
For my son, Steven,
who is faithfully walking in his destiny.
It's my joy to watch you grow into an incredible young
man who loves the Lord.

Acknowledgments

From CaSandra

Praise God from whom all blessings flow. I am who I am because of who He is.

I can't thank Him enough for the gift of writing. I'm so grateful that He continues to use me as He sees fit.

Love to my parents who tell everybody that they know that their daughter is an author.

Thanks to Michelle Stimpson my co author, prayer partner, mentor, role model and friend. I thank God for you and I love your spirit. You're always there to encourage me and I love the fact that you always have a scripture for me to stand on when I feel like I'm falling apart. You're indeed a true woman of God. Love you sis!

Special thanks to my husband Richard who has stood by my side through this writing journey. Thanks for always having my back and reading my stories. You totally rock and for that I love you babe.

I have to also thank my circle of friends, prayer partners and my Griggs Chapel Missionary Baptist Church family for your continued support.

Special, special, special thanks to you the readers. I truly appreciate all of your love and support!

From Michelle

Thank You, Lord, for re-teaching me even as I wrote this book, that our integrity is never for sale. So often, You are so faithful to have me write what I need to learn. I don't know how You do what You do, but it is marvelous in my eyes!

Thanks to CaSandra for pushing me to keep writing when I feel like, "Okay, I've written a lot of books already!"

Thanks to my grandmother, who gave us the idea for this book. Thanks to Denise, who gave me advice that curbed a scene in this book, and to my husband for information about shooting dice—it's a long story!

Thanks to my family for their support. And to my readers—I love you! You all are such an encouragement to me! Whether you're with a book club or a lone, avid reader, I really appreciate you!

Chapter 1

Willie Dale Lee, Jr. stared down at the obituary bearing his father's picture. If he kept his head down, people would hopefully deduce that he was not in the mood for a hug or a churchy cliché. They could move on down the pew to his mother and Aunt Galatia after viewing the body.

The Sunrise and Sunset dates printed beside the oval-shaped photograph seemed unreal. His father's birthday, June 12, was always a day of celebration in their household. Since it came in the summer, the family had always been able to take time and give it due honor.

The Sunset date: September 3. Just the previous week. Willie had been almost asleep when his mother called, crying frantically, screaming that his father wouldn't wake up. The ambulance was on the way.

Willie hadn't made it to the other side of Pecan Forest before the paramedics rushed his father off to the county hospital, where he was pronounced dead on arrival despite efforts to revive him with manual CPR and a defibrillator.

Willie Dale Lee, Sr. was dead.

Willie Jr. had almost thought he would find a sense of relief with his father gone. Now, he wouldn't have to hear his father say, "Willie Jr., you're going to make me real proud one day. God said it and I believe it."

Willie Jr. didn't believe it, though. Or maybe he just

didn't believe that he and his father had the same ideas about what would make a father proud of his only child.

"Will-laaay," a voice from the past said his name with the same emphasis on the last syllable.

Slightly humored, Willie looked up to see his high school football coach's wrinkled but still friendly face.

"Coach Brown. Thank you for coming." Willie hugged the man who had been like a second father throughout high school.

"Wouldn't have missed it. Got most of the offensive line here, too."

Willie glanced at the next several men in black suits. Michael Blaylock, Kirk Newsome, and James Shmidt...the faces had hardly aged in the twenty-one years they had graduated from Pecan Forest High School. Or maybe they had, but Willie was so old, too, that he didn't recognize the changes.

One by one, Willie's classmates expressed their condolences with nods, quick embraces, and pats on the back.

Willie fought to hold back tears. These guys and their support meant so much to him. They had weathered four years of hard, tough football practices in the hot Texas heat together. Their senior year, they had gone all the way to the state play-offs and would have won if the refs on the other team had stopped the clock when they were supposed to. Two more plays would have put them in field goal range, but the referee didn't see the quarterback calling time-out until they'd lost six seconds already.

They had all cried like babies on the bus ride home. When they had returned to Pecan Forest, Willie's father had been waiting in his pick-up at the school parking lot. He congratulated Willie on a good finish to his football career. Then he said, "Son, now that football is in the past, I believe it's time to be about your Father's business."

Willie knew that scripture. He knew a ton of scriptures, being the pastor's son, but he had wished his father could let him process the devastating loss before talking about church. He had wished that his father could be proud of how far the team had gotten. But no. Instead, he'd wasted that precious moment reiterating the dream he had for his son.

He wondered if his father could see his teammates now. If he could, perhaps he would finally realize how much football had meant to him and how much they had all meant to one another. So much that these guys put aside whatever they had previously planned on a Saturday morning and came to pay their respect to a former teammate's father.

I hope you can see this, Dad.

Following the ceremony, Willie had let his wife, Brenda Lee, lead him to the church fellowship hall for the repast dinner. The burial was to take place the following Monday at Mills Branch National Cemetery.

This—the eating, the socializing—was what Willie

had dreaded most. Both the service and the Repast had been held at Ebenezer Baptist instead of his father's church, Lee Chapel, because there wouldn't have been enough room to host all the family, friends, and ministerial comrades.

Yet, Ebenezer's kitchen was still too small. Even if it had been bigger, Willie wouldn't have felt comfortable with all these people eating and laughing and talking the same as if they'd just attended a wedding.

He leaned over to his wife's ear. "Brenda, I want to leave."

"No. You can't. All these people are here to support us," she whispered through a fake smile.

Willie shook his head. *How are they supporting me by eating?* "I can't stay in here. It's too stuffy."

Brenda tried to grab his hand with her dainty, well-manicured hands, but he got away before she could pull him down. "I'll be back."

Willie hoisted a fake smile of his own to his face and nodded to the sea of people who were giving proper "We're so sorry about this," and "Let the Lord comfort you," as he walked by.

He minded his manners and thanked them for their concern. When he finally reached the door, Willie flung it open, rushed down the three stairs and around the side where no one parked because there was only a thin strip of land next to a field of cows.

Finally, he could breathe. Willie closed his eyes and

inhaled deep breaths. He loosened his navy blue tie.

My father is dead.

The realization hit him for the thousandth time. He and his father disagreed about everything from the O.J. Simpson trial to whether or not men should wear pink shirts, but none of that mattered now. He was gone.

For the first time in his forty years, Willie felt unprotected. As though, up until now, there had been fences around him, keeping all the worst-case-scenarios at bay.

Not anymore. It seemed anything could happen to him without a father.

Willie figured all he could do at this point was ask the Big Man Upstairs to let his father be his guardian angel.

"Willie Jr.?" The voice belonged to Assistant Pastor Grady Sanders. His father's right-hand-man in the ministry.

Willie didn't have the strength to turn his body away from the field. Instead, he stayed facing the cows, watching them chew the grass, wishing his own life could be as plain and calm as an animal's. He felt the hand on his shoulder.

"I know, son. It's a hard day when a man says good-bye to his father."

Willie couldn't hold back the tears any longer. He let them fall as Grady stood beside him.

"Your father was a good man. Hard-working. Fair. Smart. Upright. Don't find too many like him anymore.

I'm gonna miss my friend." His voice shrank to a whisper.

A hard lump formed in Willie's throat. The only thing worse that crying in front of Pastor Grady would be Pastor Grady crying in front of him.

The older man cleared his throat. "One good thing about it, though. We know where your father is. He's resting with the Lord now."

"Yeah," Willie managed to say. "That's good."

Grady grasped Willie's shoulder firmly.

Willie faced him.

"Son, your father loved you dearly. He believed with all his heart that the Lord would use you in the ministry someday. I hate that he didn't live to see it come to pass, but I want you to know that I'm here to help you in any way as you endeavor to keep that dream alive."

There was no easy way to break the bad news to Grady, and there would probably be no better time, so Willie decided to tell his truth now. "Pastor Grady, that was my father's dream, not mine."

Pastor Grady was silent for a moment. He tipped his head to show respect, which was more than Willie had ever gotten from his own father.

They faced the cows again. Pastor Grady asked, "What is *your* dream?"

Willie had nothing to lose. "I wanted to be a rapper."

"A what?"

"A rapper. Hip-hop. Music."

"You mean like Jay X?"

Willie chuckled. "Jay *Z*."

"Oh. Tell me somethin'," Grady mumbled.

"Well…you been working toward that dream?"

"I-I mean, I listen to a lot of music," Willie said. "Keep up with the latest hits, you know?"

Grady nodded. "Yeah. You been in the studio?"

"Naw. The best studios are real expensive. I don't want to make a cheap-sounding demo. I want *the best*. Brenda says that's not in our budget, though."

"What's the budget?"

"I don't know."

"You lookin' for some work to help pay for it?"

"I'm working here and there. You know, odd jobs. But it's just scraps. Nothing like what I'll be making when I hit it big."

"I see."

Willie didn't like the tone of Pastor Grady's voice. "You believe in me? I mean, do you really think I can still be whatever I want to be?"

"No."

The stark answer made Willie laugh out loud. "I see why my dad liked you so much. You shoot straight."

Grady laughed, too. "I believe you can only be successful and enjoy that success when you make up your mind to be what God created you to be. You need to talk to *Him* and see what the plan is. Otherwise…well, let's not talk about the otherwise.

Just do what He says. Like the song says—all other ground is sinking sand."

Willie wasn't trying to hear those words. Why would God give him free will only to take it away? Why would God let him love hip-hop if it wasn't in his future? And if it was so important to God that Willie Jr. become a minister, why in the world would he take Willie Sr. away before it could happen?

"I'm going back inside now." Willie dismissed himself.

The last thing he needed was another lecture about using his life for the Lord when, clearly, it hadn't paid off for his father.

Chapter 2

Ephesia Lee woke up with a splitting headache. It was still hard for her to believe she had just buried her husband, Willie, a few days ago.

Laying in her king sized Victorian styled bed just didn't feel right without Willie. Ephesia was so used to Willie waking up early to watch TV, and he'd normally have a cup of coffee waiting for her on the nightstand. She rolled over to his side of the bed and buried her face in what used to be Willie's pillow. She could still smell his scent.

Lord, please tell me this is a horrible nightmare and that Willie will walk through the door in a minute. Ephesia held the pillow tight as if her life depended on it.

In an hour she'd be at the reading of her husband's will. It just didn't seem real. They were months away from celebrating their 47th wedding anniversary.

Willie Sr. had promised her that they would go on a cruise to celebrate. She had been trying for several years to take him. Ephesia had contacted the travel agency and even paid the deposit for a trip to Cozumel.

The ringing phone disturbed her thoughts. The caller ID revealed that it was her sister, Galatia.

"Hello," she answered.

"Hey, sis. I was calling to make sure you hadn't left yet. I'm going to pick you up so you won't have to ride by yourself."

"Oh no, that's okay. I won't be by myself. Willie Jr. should be here shortly."

"You know Willie ain't never on time for nothing, and besides I wanna be there for you."

"Yeah right," Ephesia murmured.

"Whatcha say?"

"Oh nothing. Let me go. I've got to get ready. Don't bother picking me up."

"Have it your way. I'll see you there."

Ephesia hung up the phone without saying goodbye. She and Galatia had a complicated relationship. Galatia was two years older than her and was always jealous of everything Ephesia did.

When Ephesia and Willie got engaged, Galatia did everything in her power to try to break them up. Ephesia remembered that day all too well. It was a couple of weeks before her bridal shower when Galatia came to her saying she'd seen Willie with Lena May Rogers.

Lena was very beautiful, with long, silky, jet black hair and she was the perfect size; some would say she had a coke bottle figure. Every guy in Pecan Forest dreamed of dating her.

"I saw Lena in Willie's car on Jefferson by E-Z Mart," Galatia gladly reported.

"I'm sure there's a reason why she's in his car," Ephesia replied nervously.

"Yeah, the reason is that he a low down dirty snake,

and you oughta be glad I caught him before you go down the aisle with him." Galatia smacked her lips.

"You saw them in the car, that's no big deal. I am sure Willie will have a good explanation."

"Whateva. Don't let him fool you. You know Lena got a way with men."

"Well I'm not worried. Willie loves me and I'm sure it's nothing."

"Umm hmmm, we'll see." Galatia rolled her eyes.

"Yeah, we will." Ephesia put a big smile on her face and left the room.

Ephesia rushed to the phone and called Willie, and to her surprise he informed her about Lena being in the car before she could ask. Willie was taking Lena to get a battery for her car, which had stopped a few blocks away from his house.

Willie stated that he'd seen Latia (the name he affectionately called her), and knew she'd turn it into something else.

To Galatia's dismay, Willie and Ephesia got married, and a few years later had their one and only son, Willie Jr. Galatia had gone through two husbands, with no children, and was now on her third husband who just couldn't seem to do things right.

As Ephesia looked through her closet for something to wear, she couldn't help but see Willie's clothes as well. He had a system as to how his clothes were hanging up. Regular wear clothes in the front, casual clothes in the middle, and church suits in the back.

Ephesia felt her tears coming. As much as she tried to hold it in, the pain came out like an uproar from her throat and she fell to her knees and sobbed like a baby. She had spent most of the funeral trying to be strong for her son, and for the church. She moaned like a wounded cat and began to pray. *Lord, I need Your strength, I need You to pick me up and carry me through this process, Lord, I love my husband but I know You loved him best. Please Lord, help me. You are my rock, and I run to You today, believing that You will lift this heavy burden that I feel in my heart. In Jesus name, Amen.*

Collecting herself, she got up and selected a sky blue Lord & Taylor pant suit to put on. Willie Jr. was nowhere to be found. She hadn't seen or heard from him since the burial. Ephesia knew that his father's sudden death had taken a toll on him and knew that it was going to take time for him as well as herself to heal.

Ephesia finished getting dressed and found the keys to the Cadillac CTS Sedan. *Guess I'll be driving myself.* She sighed. Willie had purchased the car for her birthday. The truth of the matter was that he drove her around in it. It wasn't that she wasn't comfortable driving it, she just loved for him to chauffer her around.

The Law Office of Morgan & Drake was about ten minutes away from Ephesia's house. The small town of Pecan Forest only had three law offices.

Ephesia pulled into the parking lot and sat there for

a minute. Reality was sinking in deeper. She was really about to hear her husband's final wishes. She took a deep breath and got out of the car.

Ephesia walked into the small office. It was very modest with floral wallpaper.

"Good morning. I'm Ephesia Lee and I'm here to see—"

"Attorney Drake," the receptionist interrupted her. "The others are already in the conference room. They're waiting on your arrival. Follow me."

"Oh okay," she said as she followed the receptionist.

Waiting for her in the conference room was Galatia, her husband, Joseph, and Pastor Grady Sanders. They were all seated at a large, round conference table. Ephesia was hoping that Willie Jr. would have been in the count but to her disappointment he wasn't there.

"Where is Willie Jr.? I thought you were riding with him?" Galatia blurted out.

"I am sure he'll be here soon. It's only 9:20; we were supposed to begin at 9:30."

"He's probably running a little behind. I talked to him earlier so he should be here shortly," Pastor Sanders added, causing Ephesia's nerves to settle down.

Attorney Drake entered the room with a file in his hands and Ephesia felt her heart beating fast. She clasped her hands together to keep them from shaking. Willie Jr. entered the room and the door slammed,

19

causing everyone to jump. He sat next to his mother and placed his arm around her.

"Good morning. Now that you all are here, we can proceed. As you already know I am Attorney Calvin Drake and I'm handling the last will and testament of Willie Dale Lee, Sr. Mrs. Lee, I offer my deepest condolences to you and your family."

Ephesia nodded.

"Mr. Lee decided to leave his wishes on DVD. I also have the notarized, legalized documents for you as well, Mrs. Lee."

Ephesia braced herself because she had no idea Willie had even created a DVD.

Attorney Drake must have noticed her uneasiness. "Mrs. Lee, let me know when you're ready and I'll start the DVD."

"You can go ahead and start it now," she managed to say.

Attorney started the DVD and Willie Sr. appeared wearing a black suit, with a white shirt and red tie.

Ephesia stared at the screen with tears in her eyes.

"I. Willie Dale Lee, Sr., being of sound mind and body declare that this is my last will and testament. My darling dearest Ephesia, I want you to know that I'll love you forever and always. If it were up to me, I'd still be home in my favorite chair watching Wheel of Fortune with you. God decided to call me home early and whatever He does He does it for His glory. To Him be all of the glory because I know where I'm going.

Ephesia, to you I leave our estate. You'll also get a check from the military every month until the day you meet me in glory. My services and burial was covered under the insurance that we both had together. Because of my love for you, I took out another policy and Attorney Drake will make sure you get the check from that as well. I love you, my darling."

"Love you, too," Ephesia whispered and searched her purse for a Kleenex.

"Willie Jr., son, I want you to know that I'm proud of you. You've come a long way and I know God has His hands on you. I just need you to grab ahold of His hand and tighten your grip. Son, I'm leaving you the Ford F150. It's paid for so you won't have to worry about a car note. All you have to do is get you some insurance. Willie, do not sell the truck. You'll also receive five thousand dollars every two years."

"Every two years, you can't be serious. I know you left me more than that?" Willie Jr. questioned as if his dad could hear him.

"Of course I left you more than that," Willie Sr. answered on cue.

"You have a lump sum waiting on you after you take the position as Senior Pastor of Lee Chapel. Now I know you don't think you have it in you to be the Pastor, but God has shown me that you will and since I know His word won't return void I'm giving you six months with Pastor Sanders help to make it work. I love you, son, and please take care of your mother."

21

"This is unbelievable. Are you sure he was in his right mind? Galatia asked.

"Galatia, I won't let you disrespect my husband." Ephesia gave her a look as to say *I'm not playing with you.*

"Shall we continue?" Attorney Drake asked. He'd paused the DVD during Galatia's outburst.

"Yes, please do," Ephesia answered.

Attorney Drake pushed the Play button on the DVD player.

"Grady, man we've been through so much. You've been a brother to me. To you I leave my boat, my fishing rods, and my hunting gear. Grady, I expect you to act as Interim Pastor of Lee Chapel until Junior is ready to take over. Grady, keep your eyes on him and make sure he does the right thing. Thanks man. You take care."

"Okay, I will, Willie." Pastor Sanders shook his head.

"To my sister-in-law, Galatia. Latia, Ephesia is going to need you in the months to come so please do whatever you can to be there for her. Latia, I know how you love African American history so to you I leave a copy of Bishop Ray Campbell's African American History Bible. There are a few people in there that I have never heard of. It's a large print King James Bible. I figured you'd be able to use it for the Black History Program that you do at the church."

"A Bible? I got dressed and came down here to hear

that I'm getting a Bible? This right here ain't even funny," Galatia fussed.

"To my brother-in-law, Joseph, it's my prayer that you will continue your role at the church as Deacon and that you will do everything asked of you to help the church continue to move forward. To you I leave my lawnmower and my barbecue pit. I've had your barbecue and it's some of the best I've ever tasted. You should seriously consider opening up a barbecue shack. I think it would be great if you started off small, maybe try to cater some events and go from there. You've also kept your yard looking pretty nice; maybe you can start a landscaping business. These are just a few ideas to help you get something a little more stable going in your life."

"Thanks a lot, Willie," Joseph said rudely.

"Well family, that's the conclusion of my will and testament. Ephesia, let God be your strength, and remember I love you forever and always."

The screen went black and Willie Sr. was gone.

Ephesia sat there looking at the screen wishing she could see him again.

"Mama, you alright?"

"I'm okay, son," she managed to say.

"Look here, Attorney Drake, do I really have to do what my father requested to get my lump sum?"

"Yes, you have to do exactly what it says otherwise you won't receive it."

"Aww man! There's got to be another way," Willie

23

Jr. said.

"Unfortunately, this is the only way."

"Well, looks like you won't be getting no money; just that measly five thousand dollars every two years." Galatia laughed.

"He'll get what's due to him because Willie is going to make his dad and I proud. He's going to take Lee Chapel to the next level. I have faith in him and I know he can do it," Ephesia said, defending her son.

The truth of the matter was that she didn't know if Willie Jr. could step up and be the Pastor or not, but she was going to do everything in her power to make sure that he did.

Chapter 3

Galatia Dewhickey was livid. She couldn't believe that her brother-in-law had the audacity to leave her a Bible. She knew their relationship wasn't the greatest but that shouldn't have mattered. She was still part of his family.

"I can't believe Willie didn't leave the church to you, honey. You're way more capable of running things than Junior," Galatia said as she washed dishes.

"You know Willie didn't like me. I'm surprised he left me anything," Joseph replied.

"He ordained you as a Deacon so that ought to count for something," she pointed out.

"Baby, the only reason I'm a Deacon is because you insisted on me being one," he reminded her.

"Well, you should be glad that I did. You deserve a position in the church. You could be the next Pastor of Lee Chapel."

"The name of the church is *Lee* Chapel not Dewhickey, which means that Willie wanted to keep it in the family since he's the founder."

"Whose side are you on?" She sighed.

"Look, I'm always on your side. Stop worrying. I got something I'm working on. We will be alright. It's going to work out," he said, pulling Galatia close to him, giving her a hug and a passionate kiss. He swatted her on her bottom and went into the den.

Galatia felt like she was floating on a cloud every

time Joseph touched her. She thought back to how they first met. She and Joseph meet at a car wash. At the time, he was working there. He'd washed and waxed up her BMW; had it looking brand new. Galatia gave him a tip and he flirted with her and gave her his card. After getting her car detailed seven times, Joseph finally asked her out on a date.

Galatia accepted and agreed to meet him for dinner. She got all dolled up, wearing a sheer multicolored sundress and a pair of strappy sandals. She met him at Red Lobster. Dating was something she hadn't done in a while. She had vowed that she was through with men after her last divorce. She'd been married twice.

Once Galatia arrived at the restaurant, she'd spotted Joseph sitting at the bar and joined him. Joseph looked great in his jeans and button down shirt. Tall, dark, and very handsome, he could pass as Morris Chestnut's twin.

"Hey pretty lady." He stood and greeted her.

"Hey handsome." She blushed.

"I'm so glad you decided to have dinner with me, I wanted to ask you out when I first met you."

"Really? Why me?"

"Why not you? You're beautiful, got your little jazzy look going on. You got it going on."

"Well, thank you. I've never had anyone say that to me."

"That means you been hanging around the wrong cats." He grabbed her hand and kissed it.

"Joseph, how old are you?"

"Old enough to treat you right, and take care of you like you need to be taken care of." He flashed her a smile like he'd just hit the jackpot.

"Seriously, Joseph. I'm 64 years old. What could you possibly want from me?" she questioned.

"I don't want anything from you, just to get to know you. I'm looking for a wife."

"So you've never been married? Do you have any children?"

"I've never been married, and as far as I know I don't have any children."

"Really? That's rare. So tell me now, Joseph, how old are you?"

"I'm 38, but age is mind over matter. If you don't mind, it don't matter."

"You could be my son. What will people say?"

"They'll say, that sure is a nice looking couple." He flashed his smile at her again.

That was all it took to convince Galatia. She and Joseph got married six months later and things had been going downhill since then. Joseph assumed that Galatia had money since she drove a BMW. Little did he know that the BMW was her sister's old vehicle that she passed on to her.

Galatia had retired from the local newspaper, The Pecan Forest Herald. She had worked there since she graduated high school. Her home was paid for, so her income was really just enough to take care of her. She had no idea that she would have to take care of Joseph, too.

Shortly after Joseph said "I do" to Galatia, he said "I *don't*" to work. It was as if he was a different person. He got fired from the carwash and every now and then he'd pick up a job here and there but nothing stable.

Of course Ephesia and Willie weren't surprised because they didn't think Galatia should have married him. Galatia recalled that day when she called Ephesia to give her the news.

"Good news, Ephesia. I'm getting married," she sang.

"Married? To who?"

"What do you mean, to who?" she said irritated.

"You can't seriously be thinking about marrying Joseph. You don't really know him," Ephesia pointed out.

"I know that he loves me and I love him."

"Love? How can you be in love so quickly?"

"You can't put a time minimum on love. When it's real, you know it."

"Galatia, look, I know that you're quite fond of him but he's too young for you. Don't you know young men like Joseph prey on older women? They make them feel like they're sitting on top of the world and then they tear up your world. That's what happened to Effie May Patterson. She married that young guy and he took everything she had; that's why she moved to Richardson with her children. I'm telling you, Galatia, these guys are looking for their next cougar."

"Well, I'm not worried because Joseph is different. He cares about me for real. Why can't you just be happy for me?" she yelled.

"Galatia, I want you to be happy but I just honestly don't think he's the one for you. I don't trust him."

"You don't have to trust him. I trust him. Maybe you're just a little jealous of my relationship with Joseph."

"That's absurd. Why would I be jealous? I have my own husband."

"Yeah you have a husband. It's always been *Ephesia* got a husband, *Ephesia* got a nice brick home, *Ephesia* got a nice car, *Ephesia, Ephesia, Ephesia.* I'm sick of being in the shadows. It's my turn now; my turn to have some joy, excitement, and love in my life," she cried.

"Galatia, this isn't about me. I won't apologize for the life that I have. I'm not against you. You're my sister and I just want what's best for you. If you feel like this is the best decision then you go right on."

That's exactly what Galatia and Joseph did. They flew to Vegas and got married. Galatia of course paid for everything, even went to Thompson's Jewelry and opened an account to get them some wedding rings.

After two years of marriage things still weren't going great. Joseph was always out late, claiming to be working with one of his friends but he never had any money to show for it. Every now and then he'd give

Galatia $100 but those times were few and far between. That's why Galatia wished Willie would have left her some money. It wasn't like he couldn't afford too.

"Baby? Baby, did you hear me calling you?" Joseph asked, bringing her back to reality.

"Huh? What you say? Sorry I must have been daydreaming."

"Give me Junior's number. I need to holla at him about something."

Galatia rattled off the number and finished cleaning the kitchen.

Joseph went into their bedroom, retrieved his cell phone, and dialed Junior's number.

"Junior, what's cracking?"

"Man, not much. Just left my mom's house to check on her. What's going on?"

"I've got a plan to help you make Lee Chapel the most prosperous church in Pecan Forest."

"Plan? What kinda plan?" he inquired.

"Man, look, it's complicated and I don't really want to talk about it on the phone. Do you have access to the church?"

"Yeah, I have the key, if that's what you're talking about."

"Okay cool. Let's meet up at the church and I'll give you all the details there."

"Joseph, this ain't no scam or nothing, is it?"

"Naw, man. This ain't no scam. It's legit, and once we get things rolling you won't have to worry about just getting that five thousand every two years. This is going to help you out financially until you start getting your salary for being the Pastor."

"Man, I don't want to be no Pastor. I want to use my money for some studio time. I got some fellas in Atlanta waiting for me to cut a single."

"Studio time? Man you got to be the Pastor to get the money. I see you haven't put a lot of thought into it, which is another reason why you need to meet me at the church."

"Joseph, look man, I'll meet you there in about an hour, but I'm not interested in doing nothing that will get me into trouble. I'm really trying to get myself on track. I just got this warehouse gig through the temp service. You might can get on, too. They need some extra help."

"Naw, man, I don't do warehouse work, but anyway you gon' meet me or not?" Joseph said, getting to the matter at hand.

"Yeah, I guess I'll meet you at 5:30. I don't have nothin' to lose."

"Alright bet," Joseph said. He hung up the phone and did a little dance. He was ready to put his plan in full effect.

Chapter 4

Whatever his Uncle Joseph had in mind couldn't be good. Willie knew this as sure as taxes and death. But if there was money involved, he would at least listen because $5000 every two years wasn't going to cut it. Willie needed steady income, or at least a 5-figure lump sum, to make Brenda happy.

"Get your feet off the coffee table," Brenda fussed as she flung his feet off the composite wood.

"Watch out there, girl!" he teased her as she dusted the furniture. Watching his wife's curvy backside swish from side to side without the effort suddenly roused long-dormant feelings. Underneath the long skirts and turtlenecks, Brenda was as fine as any fitness guru. Willie ran a hand along her hip.

She quickly swatted him. "Stop!" Her brown eyes flashed with anger.

"A man can't touch his wife?"

"A man who's got time to sit and watch television in the middle of the workday needs to be looking for a *job* instead of flirting."

"I *have* a job," Willie argued. "Starting next week."

"A *temporary* job." Brenda put a hand on her hip. "But our bills are *permanent*. Regular and *permanent*. And a lot can change before next week. For all we know, you might get fired before you ever show up."

"Woman, I'm about to put five thousand dollars in

our checking account as soon as the lawyer cuts my check!"

"You think five thousand dollars makes up for three years of me working myself to the bone to support you? Five thousand dollars is a drop in the bucket. And your father would have left you more if you'd had anything going for you."

Willie pouted as he left the living room and entered their bedroom, slamming the door behind him.

Brenda never failed to somehow relate everything to the fact that Willie didn't have a steady job. If he asked her for a piece of bread, she'd ask, "What you makin'—an unemployment sandwich?"

They'd been living off her nursing assistant's paycheck and whatever Willie could earn when the temporary services found him work. His dad used to hook him up with jobs around town, too. There weren't many job opportunities in Pecan Forest, TX. People with good jobs held on to them for dear life. Didn't help that he was black. And with the main textile factory closing three years ago, the town had all but dried up. Had it not been for his father's occasional bail-out, Willie and Brenda would have been homeless a long time ago.

As Willie laid back on the bed, surfing through the television channels, he grew even angrier. Brenda was one of the lucky ones who had found stable work in Pecan Forest. She had no idea how demoralizing and humiliating it was to go from business to business for months and months filling out applications, being questioned in interviews, and later told you'd done all that for nothing. Wasting his time. Treating him like less than a human being.

Come to think of it, he was tired of Brenda treating him badly, too. When they'd first married, Brenda was kind. Sweet. Willie had been working at the bank, thanks to a favor from his father's friend, for nearly nine months. He had a steady cell phone number, a checking account, and a car with real insurance. For the first time since he was in high school, Willie seemed to be on the right track again.

He moved out of his parents' house to Brenda's apartment, which caused a rift between Willie and his parents. They still loved him, but they reminded him every chance they got that he was living in sin and they wouldn't support him in any way so long as he was out of line with the Lord.

Willie didn't care. He was in love. Brenda's pretty brown face and her smart, ambitious, church-going ways, he couldn't lose. He'd have a beautiful wife and someone who knew how to pray for him in his corner— nothing could go wrong.

But then Willie's car broke down. He couldn't get to work on time. He took out a loan to get the car fixed. As soon as he fixed it, somebody stole it. That's when he learned that he only had "liability" insurance. Whoever stole the car didn't live anywhere near Pecan Forest—Willie knew because he had searched up and down every street. They'd gotten away scot-free.

Without reliable transportation, Willie wasn't able to keep the job. He couldn't keep any job without a ride. That's when he started scheduling work at temporary services on Brenda's off days.

That's also about the time when Brenda started to pull away from him. She was angry. Complaining. Fussing about having to "carry" him. Willie wanted to move back home, but his parents actually cared about Brenda and wanted the two of them to get married.

Even Aunt Galatia had gotten in on the action. "You love her, don't you, son?" She had cornered him one day after church.

"Of course I do."

"Then make an honest woman out of her and maybe God'll give you another job," she had said before stomping off to meet her precious Joseph in the parking lot.

If his Aunt Galatia and Uncle Joseph could stay married, surely he and Brenda could.

They married at the courthouse because Willie Sr. made it a principle not to hold church weddings for people who were already living together. Willie, Jr. did see a change in his father's attitude after Brenda was made an "honest woman." Willie Jr. had hoped that Brenda's attitude would change once he gave her his last name. He was wrong. Brenda wanted a paycheck more than "Lee."

Willie sighed now, settling on a reality TV show

about women who were addicted to plastic surgery. *Ridiculous.*

He wondered if Brenda would be like that if and when he got rich. Would she do something to her nose? She used to say she thought her nose was too wide, but Willie had always thought it was perfect. Regal. Just like every part of her appearance. He missed seeing her thick lips smile, though. He wondered if, underneath all the worries about paying bills and the long hours at the nursing home, his old Brenda was still in there. He missed her and it seemed the only way to get her back was to get some money.

Maybe the meeting with Joseph would be the key to saving his self-respect. His marriage. His life.

Willie sat alone in the church office studying the barely-present spine of his father's large-print leather King James Bible. He took a deep breath. Silently flipped through. Almost every page was bathed in marks and highlights, dates, notes and arrows. His father had been a student of the Bible. Willie never could figure out how a person could read the same passages of scriptures over and over again, but his father had done it. And *lived* it.

"Knock, knock!"

Willie turned to see Joseph entering the room. "Hey."

"Hello to you, too. What you doing—looking for

twenty dollar bills tucked in the pages of your daddy's Bible?"

"Naw. I was just waiting for you."

"Well, I'm here now so let's get to business." Joseph closed the Bible as he sat across from Willie. "Put the good book away. Don't wanna get struck by lightning."

Willie obeyed, sliding the Bible into a desk drawer. "Are we about to set the church on fire for the insurance money or something?" Willie laughed.

Joseph's eyes twinkled for a moment, then he said, "That's not what I had in mind. But I like the way you think, nephew."

Willie wanted to tell Joseph that he was only kidding, but Joseph took the conversation away.

"Here's the deal. I have a friend. Earnest. He works at the race tracks in Grand Prairie. He's been studying the horses, studying the races for months. *Months!*"

Willie watched as Joseph's face practically glowed with a contagious excitement.

"They got a race coming up. Earnest has already been studying the horses. He won five hundred dollars last week, and he's got a sure-fire winner coming up Monday. Misty Blue."

"Misty Blue?"

"Yeah. That's the horse's name. The odds are against him, partly because he's not a thoroughbred. But Earnest told me all about this horse and his competition. Misty Blue is the one to put our money on."

"*Our* money?"

"Yeah. The five thousand dollars."

"I have to put that money in my joint account with Brenda."

Joseph leaned in more across the desk. "Look. This is just the first run. We can start small. Say, two thousand dollars. Can you break off that much until after the race? You'll put it right back in the account when we win, plus some. Or you can just keep all the extra money for yourself. What Brenda don't know won't hurt her."

The idea of having extra money for himself—apart from all the bill-paying Brenda allocated his funds for—was enticing. He could buy more studio time. Get a fake gold tooth and a snake tattoo and have his hair braided. If he wanted to contend with these young hip-hop stars, he needed to look the part.

There was only one problem. "I don't have the check yet."

"Shoot!" Joseph pounded his fist on the desk. "When will you have it?"

"Wednesday, at the earliest."

"Man. Misty Blue races Monday. We need the money *Monday*."

"No can do," Willie said.

A smile spread across Joseph's face. "We could use…the offering?"

"The offering?"

"Yeah. Sunday's offering," Joseph repeated.

"The church's money?" Willie clarified.

Joseph nodded.

"I don't know about that."

"*I* know you need more than five thousand dollars every few years. And *I* know your father's gone so you're about to be stuck like Chuck so your security blanket is gone. You gotta start a business, get some kind of side hustle going or something. And it *takes* money to *make* money."

This whole thing sounded crazy to Willie. But he couldn't come down on Joseph too hard because Willie's hands weren't entirely clean. Over the years, he had "borrowed" money here and there from the offering plate. He always put it back, though, whenever he got a paycheck. *This wouldn't be any different, right?*

Willie's hands shook even as he thought about this idea. "I—I don't think so, Joseph. I'm going to try to make it happen with this first installment."

"Suit yourself. But don't hate on me when I'm riding around in my Escalade and you still put-puttin' around trying to find a job in this God-forsaken city." Joseph stood. "I'm out."

Chapter 5

"Hallelujah! Hallelujah! I love to praise His name!"
The choir sang as Willie and the other trustees tapped
their feet on the pews to the right of the platform.

As a child, Willie had watched the deacons occupy
this designated spot and wondered how they got to sit
so close to his father during the Sunday service. Now
that he was sitting on the row, he wondered if there was
actually anything special about being a deacon, an
elder, or anything people looked up to. Willie was on
the advisory board of Lee Chapel's Sunday school.
Something his father made up in order to have Willie
listed amongst church leadership. But, truth be told, all
Willie did was order the Sunday school books once
quarterly.

Willie glanced down his row and saw Joseph
raising his hands in praise. The same hands that,
according to Joseph's phone call the previous evening,
had flown straight up in the air when Misty Blue came
in first place. Joseph had taken some money from Aunt
Galatia's account at the last minute and bet on his
friend's prediction.

"Willie, I won six times what I put in! You hear
me—*six times*! Put the money back in Galatia's account
before she could miss it. I know your Daddy frowned
on gambling, but you a *fool* not to bet on a sure thing,
Willie."

He had ended the conversation with Joseph abruptly as regret inched up his spine. Then he remembered that all he had to his name was twelve dollars. Even if he had bet everything he'd had, twelve times six wasn't enough to buy an hour in a premier studio.

The choir repeated the familiar chorus several times as many in the church began to "get happy", yelling and singing along. Sometimes, Willie wished he could get excited like them. But church had always been something they *did*. This whole idea of getting emotional over a God he couldn't see—Willie couldn't imagine it.

But he did like what he saw coming through the front door of the church. A tall, slim woman in a skin-tight red dress with bare legs and skinny heels.

Almost instantly, the church seemed to focus on her. Even Riley, the choir director, glanced behind his shoulder to see what had taken the choir members' attention from his flailing arms. Riley must have liked what he saw, too, because the choir was stuck on "I love to praaaaaaaaaaa—" as he took a second and third take of the woman.

Mother Smith, on the piano, brought the song on in without Riley's help.

"His holy name!" The choir finally stopped.

Willie stood and clapped. Not because he'd been moved by the Spirit, but in order to get a better view of the woman's backside as she shuffled down the third row to take a seat.

41

She happened to sit a few feet away from Brenda.

When Willie's eyes accidentally crossed his wife's smoldering glare, he knew he'd allowed his assessment of the visitor to linger too long.

He clapped harder. "Amen and amen!"

Following the song, the church's announcement clerk, Sister Hattie Lou Willis, took the side podium. Her pillbox hat and pin-striped suit were straight out of the 1960s. So old it was probably back in style.

After reminding the members of weekly meetings, Sister Hattie Lou asked all the visitors to stand.

Willie paid close attention as the woman in red announced, "Hello. My name is Courtney Frazier. I'm new to Pecan Forest. Originally from Sweet Lily, Texas. Thank you for your hospitality."

"Amen. *You* may be seated," Sister Hattie Lou quickly said, which was out of the norm because visitors usually stood until after they'd been greeted by at least half the church.

With no other visitors in attendance, Sister Hattie Lou gave a quick, "You are welcome, welcome, welcome," and turned the service back over to the pulpit. There would be no hugging on Miss Courtney Frazier thanks to Sister Hattie Lou.

Willie endured the rest of the service. He turned to the scriptures and read along as Grady preached. This was only the second Sunday since Willie's father had passed. It wasn't unusual to hear Grady preach a Sunday sermon, but twice in a row was unusual. Willie would try to get used to it, but for now, he couldn't. He couldn't imagine that he'd never hear his father preach again.

Forty-five minutes later, Grady was making the altar call. As usual, no one came down the aisle to give their lives to Jesus. Presumably, everyone in the building was already saved. If they weren't, they surely wouldn't want to announce it at this point.

Church was dismissed. Willie shook hands will his fellow leaders. Joseph, of course, winked at him and said, "You missin' out."

"I get my check Wednesday."

"Okay. I'll let you know when's the next big race."

Despite his feelings about church and the God who had taken his father back to heaven, Willie still didn't like the idea of discussing gambling in the sanctuary.

He left Joseph's presence and stopped to hug his mother before meeting up with Brenda in the parking lot.

To his surprise, Brenda wasn't mingling with members. She was already in the car sitting in the driver's seat. Engine going, windows rolled up as though she was making every effort to avoid fraternizing.

Willie said "good-bye" and thanked the members who were still offering condolences. He joined Brenda on the passenger's side. "What's up?"

"Did you seriously follow that woman to her seat? And did you seriously look at her every five seconds during the sermon?"

Did I? He didn't think it was every five seconds. Sure, it was frequent. But not ever five seconds. "Brenda, it's human nature to look closely at someone you've never seen before."

"You are so full of lies!" She shrieked. "What did Rev. Grady preach about?"

Willie tried the obvious. "Jesus."

"What *about* Jesus?"

"Ummm…He's the rose of Sherrod."

"No!"

"Bright and morning star?"

"Noooo!" Brenda burst into tears. "You think life is one big joke, don't you, Willie?"

His heart raced at the sight of his wife crying. He could handle a whole lot of disappointment and even physical pain—but this one nearly outdid him every time. "Brenda, honey, don't cry." He reached for her chin.

She pushed his hand away. "You leave me no choice," she said, sniffing. "I'm leaving you, Willie."

"What?" He put a hand on the gears to keep her from driving. "What do you mean, you're leaving?"

"I am. I actually had my bags packed a few weeks ago. But then your father died, and I didn't want to leave you at your lowest moment. So I stayed—halfway hoping that losing him would somehow make you mature. Hoping that his dreams for you to become a minister would become your dream, too. But I see I was wrong. You're never going to change. You'll always be Willie Lee Jr.—the preacher's *kid* who never became a *man*."

Willie wished he could refute her words. He wished he could counter her argument. But he couldn't. Everything she said only confirmed his worst fear—he was a loser in every sense of the word.

Willie didn't try to stop Brenda from leaving when they got home. She packed two suitcases and left without another word while Willie sat on the couch pretending to watch the football game.

His favorite team was getting blown-out by the opponent. And so was he.

Depositing the check for five thousand dollars should have been one of the happiest moments of Willie's life. He didn't have any immediate plans for the money. He could spend it all in the studio. Make a down payment on one of the best producers. Then again, five thousand didn't go far in the music industry.

Joseph put a few more bugs in his ear about Misty Blue.

"Wait until the weekend," was Willie's reply. Truth was, Willie wasn't in the mood to lust over money.

He missed Brenda. He'd even called her the second the deposit was complete. "Brenda, I put the money in our account."

"Okay."

"Okay…so…can we talk? Maybe go to one of those nice restaurants in the city? We've got the money for it now. We could even spend the night at one of the expensive hotels."

"You're going to need that money for the apartment rent, Willie. The lease isn't up for another three months. I'm going to take my name off the paperwork and you'll be on your own."

Brenda was talking about things that were months and months away. She really needed to learn how to live in the now. He quoted scripture, "Tomorrow has enough troubles of its own."

"Your tomorrows got a lot of trouble since you can't keep a job. You need to worry about that today. Why don't you pay the bills up and get some insurance so you can get back and forth to work? Bye."

As angry as he had been at the end of their conversation, he still missed her. He also realized that she was right. He would need to make sure that he could get to work. He called his dad's longtime friend, Copper, who owned an auto mechanic shop. Within an hour, Willie headed to the shop.

Copper had one of his trusted employees to make sure the truck was running right. Willie paid for the repairs and went to The Insurance Hub to get coverage.

Brenda usually handled the paperwork in his life. She handled everything in his life, the same way his mom had done for his father.

What am I going to do without her?

The apartment was so empty without her that Willie actually voluntarily decided to attend church Wednesday night.

And that decision turned out to be a winner because after service, he happened to bump into Miss Courtney Frazier. She was exiting the ladies' room as Willie walked out the front door.

"I don't believe we've met."

"Oh. I'm Willie Lee," he said, shaking her dainty hand.

Courtney's skin glowed with youth and perfectly orchestrated make-up. She had to be in her late twenties or so. "Willie Lee of this Lee Chapel?"

"Yes. He was my father. I'm a junior."

Courtney put a hand to her ample bosom. "I'm so sorry about your father's passing. I hear he was a great man of God."

"Thank you. He was." Willie noted her dancing eyes, the dimples in her cheeks despite the words of sympathy. She was interested in him. He knew it as sure as he'd known that every girl at Pecan Forest High School would have given anything to date him because he played football.

"Would you...like to hear more about him?"

"Certainly."

Willie ventured, "Over dinner?"

"Sure." She snapped at the bait.

Well, if Brenda don't want me, at least somebody does.

47

Chapter 6

Ephesia wasn't really in the mood to have company. Every day since Willie's death, she'd had several members from the church to stop by to offer their condolences and of course bring her some food. If it hadn't been for Junior stopping by to get food, she would have had to give it to a shelter.

Yesterday she purposely arrived to church after devotion because she knew all of the members would want to talk to her and ask her how she felt.

She honestly didn't know how she felt. One minute she felt like she was dreaming, the next minute she was numb. She wanted to simply be left alone.

When her best friend, Ruthie Nell Sanders, called saying she wanted to come by, Ephesia told her it was okay. Ruthie Nell and her husband, Grady, were she and Willie's best friends. They got married around the same time, took family trips together, celebrated birthdays and anniversaries, and they were the first ones to join Lee Chapel and, later, Grady became Willie's right-hand-man in the ministry.

Grady and Ruthie Nell were faithful members, never complained, and always willing to do whatever they could to help out. There were times in the early days when Willie didn't know if Lee Chapel would make it. With twenty members and only five or six of them paying their tithes things were rough. Grady and

Ruthie Nell offered to put up the money to help Willie pay the church off. Willie thanked them for the offer but told them that He trusted God to handle it. A month later he received a check from his Uncle's death and it was more than enough to pay the church off.

The doorbell rang and Ephesia walked down the hallway to open the door.

"Hey, sis. How you doing today?" Ruthie Nell said as she entered and hugged Ephesia. The dark circles underneath Ephesia's eyes confirmed that she hadn't been sleeping.

"I honestly don't know. Every day is a struggle," she said and sighed.

She led Ruthie Nell into the living room so they could talk.

"I can't say I know how you feel, but I will say God is going to carry you through this. We're all praying for you," Ruthie Nell said as she adjusted her skirt and sat on the leather sectional.

"I know God is able, I just wish I had more time. You know, time to prepare." Ephesia's voice shook.

"I don't think it would have made a difference. I mean think about it, if Pastor had been sick for a while, that might have been worse. You wouldn't have wanted to see him waste away, and he definitely wouldn't have wanted you to suffer through that," Ruthie Nell pointed out.

"I guess you're right. I'm just dazed right now," she confessed.

"It's alright. It'll get better with time; just gotta take things one day at a time. Let God be your strength."

"I have to be honest, I didn't feel up to having company today but I'm glad you came. You always know what to say."

"Well praise God! I'm glad to help lift your spirits."

"What did you want to talk to me about?"

"The Women's Conference is supposed to take place next weekend and Mother Clarece Edwards and Sister Margie Phelps think we should cancel it. I told them that I would talk to you before we make any decisions."

"The conference? Oh my goodness, I totally forgot. Is everything taken care of?" she inquired.

"We have everything taken care of, but we didn't know if you would want us to move forward under the circumstances."

"I appreciate your concern but the church must go on. Willie would want us to carry on as if he was still here." She struggled saying the latter part of her sentence.

Reality had hit her this morning as she sat and looked at the chair that Willie normally sat in and now saying that he was no longer here was a hard pill to swallow.

"Sis, you alright? Do you need a glass of water?" Ruthie Nell offered.

"No I'm okay. Who's scheduled to come to the conference?" she managed to ask.

"We have First Lady Catherine Oaks from Sweet Lily and First Lady Elisa Baker from Longview, Texas."

"Who is Elisa Baker? I've never heard of her?"

"That's because she just became a First Lady. She married Pastor Dewayne Baker from Truway. She's a powerful, young woman of God, been on fire for God for some years. Her father was a preacher, too. We figured it would be good to have her minister to the younger members."

"I think that's a great idea. Did you tell Brenda?"

"Brenda who?" Ruthie Nell asked.

"Brenda Lee, my daughter-in-law, who will be the next First Lady of Lee Chapel," Ephesia said confidently.

"I haven't talked to Brenda, but honestly sis, do you think this is something she would want to do? I don't mean no harm, but I've never seen Brenda at Sunday school or Bible study."

"Well, that's about to change. She's going to be more involved moving forward especially now that Junior is preparing to be the Pastor."

"Well..." Ruthie Nell hesitated, "do you really think Junior is ready?"

"I think his father saw something in Him that made him decide to leave him the church. My husband's legacy will live on through Junior and not only do I respect his decision, I trust God to work on my son," Ephesia said, trying not to upset Ruthie Nell.

"I respect Pastor's legacy and decision, too. The question is, does *Junior* respect his father's wishes? You know we've been friends for a long time and I consider you family, so I have to be truthful with you."

"Truthful with me about what?" Ephesia said louder than Ruthie Nell expected.

"I saw Junior flirting with one of the visitors yesterday and to top it off I saw him give her a piece of paper."

"What does him giving her a piece of paper have to do with this?"

"It means he was giving her his phone number," she stated matter-of-factly.

"That doesn't prove anything." Ephesia defended her only child.

"Well he certainly wasn't giving her a church bulletin and he looked like he was after her. He had pure lust in his eyes."

"Ruthie Nell, I expected this type of accusations from those little biddies at the church but not you. I can't believe you're sitting in my living room accusing Junior of trying to cheat on his wife." Ephesia huffed, her emotions running high.

"Look, I'm not trying to rattle your cage, just thought I'd let you know before you hear from someone else. I hope he's innocent. But when you see him, ask him about it."

"I most certainly will. I'm sure it's not what you think."

"Well, I better get going. I'll call Brenda and invite her to the conference as well as the upcoming meeting next week."

"Okay great, and Ruthie Nell, do me a favor. Don't tell anyone what you just told me, especially not Galatia."

"I won't tell a soul and I am going to pray that Junior will do the right thing," Ruthie Nell agreed as she headed up the hallway to leave. "Call me if you need anything. Love you."

"Love you, too," Ephesia said as she watched her walk out of the door.

Ephesia was livid. She knew Ruthie Nell wasn't lying. Ruthie wasn't the type of person that would say something just to upset you. If she said it, it was the truth.

Ephesia stormed into her bedroom and retrieved her phone to call Junior.

After the fourth ring he finally answered.

"Mom, hey. I was going to call you in a bit. How you doing today?"

"Junior, who is the girl you were flirting with at church?" she blurted out.

"Dang, Mama. Who said that? I was only speaking to Courtney. She was a visitor. I walked around and shook hands with *all* the visitors. Figured I'd welcome everyone and let them know that I am the next Pastor of the church," Willie Jr. said, hoping that would stop Ephesia from asking any additional questions.

"That better be the only thing that you were doing," Ephesia fussed.

"That's all I was doing. And who told you I was talking to Courtney? Probably ole Grady. He got the right name, too, cause he acts just like Grady on Sanford and Son."

"Who told me isn't important. You just make sure you're not caught doing something wrong, and you better hope Brenda don't find out."

"There's nothing to find out," he lied. There was no way in the world Willie could tell Ephesia that Brenda already knew and that she had left him. The last time Brenda left, she took him back the very next day and Ephesia never knew about it. He had no idea how he was going to keep the news from Ephesia or if Brenda would take him back this time.

"Junior, your father is well known in this town and in the church community. I want you to keep that in mind. Don't you do nothing to tarnish his name or the church's name. You hear me?" Ephesia cautioned him.

"I hear you, Mama. Why you always think I'm up to something?"

"Because you usually are."

"Mama, I'm innocent. You gotta believe me," Willie Jr. pleaded.

"You better be, Junior. I'll talk to you later."

Ephesia hung up the phone before he could say goodbye. She hoped that Junior was telling the truth but in her heart her motherly instinct told her differently.

Chapter 7

Brenda Lee ignored her husband's call for the fiftieth time today. She was tired of him begging and making her promises that he never kept. She loved Willie Jr. but it was time for her to show him some tough love. Showing him tough love was also tough on her.

She'd left Willie and went to stay with her sister, Diana.

Diana never liked Willie Jr. and she didn't try to hide it.

"Girl, you oughta be glad you don't have any children with that bum of a husband of yours," she said as she and Brenda put sheets on her bed in the guest room.

"Di, how could you say that? You know I've always wanted children."

"Yes and you still can have children, just not with him. He's a child himself."

"I know you don't like Willie but he's still my husband and I still love him. I don't really want a divorce. What I want is for my husband to change."

"He's showing you who he really is. Why won't you believe him?" Diana asked.

"I can't get you to understand because you've never been married. When I stood at the altar and recited my vows I meant them. I need your shoulder to lean on right now, and can you please stop disrespecting my husband?"

"Unbelievable. I can't believe you're defending someone who's selfish and couldn't care less about you. Think about it. If he really cared about you, he wouldn't have been eyeing that young girl at church and he would be over here begging you to come back home with him," Diana pointed out.

"First of all, he wouldn't come over here because he knows you don't like him and secondly, he's been calling me begging and pleading for me to come home all day. Like I said, Di, stay out of this. Thanks for letting me stay here but please keep Willie's name out of your mouth."

"Well excuse me. Someone's all in their feelings. I just hope now you'll focus on going to school to get your nursing degree so that you can make some real money. You won't have to stress over bills or worry about driving a car from the tote your note dealership."

"I'll go to school when time permits. Now if you don't mind, I need some alone time."

"Suit yourself," Diana said and left the room.

Diana lived on the outskirts of Pecan Forest in a city called Deni. Most of the residents of Deni were well off. Diana was a dentist and her office was located in the heart of Deni.

She'd graduated high school, went to college, and started her dental career. Diana had dated a few men but never had a serious relationship. She was married to her job.

Her six thousand square foot, two story, five bedroom home, and her red Lexus was all she seemed to care about. She even named her car Max and said that it was her baby.

Of course Brenda wanted a better life but she wanted a better life with her husband. She wanted her marriage to be the way God intended it to be. She scrolled through her phone and looked at pictures that she and Willie had taken on their one-year anniversary.

They looked so happy, and for the most part back then they were.

Willie treated her like she mattered and even looked at her like he was still attracted to her. Although she wasn't considered a plus size woman she sometimes felt like she was.

"What happened to us? What happened to the love we had in the beginning?" Brenda asked aloud as if she expected the picture to answer her.

The phone buzzed and the Caller ID revealed that she had an incoming call from Ruthie Nell Sanders.

I wonder what she wants, Brenda sighed, wondering if she should answer the phone.

"Hello," she answered.

"Sister Brenda, this is Ruthie Nell Sanders. How are you doing, dear?"

"I'm fine. How can I help you?"

"I was calling to tell you about our upcoming Women's Conference, I know this is all new to you but

First Lady Lee insisted that I include you since you'll be our next Lady Elect," Ruthie Nell said.

"I'm not sure if I'll be able to attend," she said, not wanting to tell Ruthie Nell her business. Clearly Willie hadn't told his mother about them separating.

"May I ask why?"

This woman got some nerves asking me why. Brenda took a few breaths before she answered her. "I'm unsure at this time, Sister Sanders, but I appreciate the invitation," she said sternly.

"Sister Brenda, I'm sensing that something's wrong. I'm here to talk and be of assistance to you if need be. I can hear the stress in your voice, sweetheart."

At that moment Brenda began to sob. She could no longer hold it in.

Ruthie Nell allowed her to sob until she was ready to talk.

"I'm so sorry, Sister Sanders. I didn't mean to cry on you." Brenda sniffed.

"That's okay. Crying cleanses the soul. We all have those moments. I meant what I said about being her for you. If you're up to talking about what is bothering you, we can do that now, and whatever we discuss will be just between us," Ruthie Nell assured her.

"I'm having issues in my marriage and I don't know what to do," Brenda blurted out.

"The problem isn't yours to solve, Brenda. It's the Lord's. There's nothing in the world too hard for Him to work out."

"You don't understand, Sister Sanders, Willie—"

"It doesn't matter what you or Willie did. That's none of my business," Ruthie Nell said, cutting Brenda off. "You young people are so quick to blab your business. That's a trick of the enemy. The enemy wants you to down-talk your husband and talk about what he's not doing. You gotta flip the script and start speaking what you wanna see. Speak positive even when you see negative and build him up. Instead of pointing out what he's *not* doing, applaud him for what he *is* doing," Ruthie Nell advised.

"That's easier said than done."

"When we do things based on how we feel, that makes things harder. Even the Bible tell us in Jeremiah 17:9 that our hearts are deceitful and wicked."

"Sister Sanders, so you mean to tell me you've never gotten upset with Rev. Sanders and vented to someone?"

"I tried to vent to my mother but she wouldn't let me. She said my marriage was between me, Grady, and God. I now know why she told me that."

"Why is that?" Brenda sat up in the bed attentively. She wanted to know what Sis. Sanders meant by all of this.

"It's because once you stop being mad and make up, the people you've told your business may still be upset with your spouse and you all ga ga goo goo over one another."

"I guess you're right." Brenda laughed.

"Sister Brenda, I've been married for 47 years and although every day hasn't been peaches and cream, I thank God for the husband He blessed me with. God is the glue that holds us together."

"That's a long time. Sometimes I don't know if I want to be married 47 minutes," Brenda confessed.

"You're going to change your language, Sis. Brenda. Remember, be positive. God specializes in restoring and rebuilding marriages. I've seen Him do it. Hold on to your faith," Ruthie Nell encouraged her.

"Yes, ma'am."

"See now you sound better. We're having Women's Bible Study this coming Thursday and I would love for you to come. I think you'll enjoy it. You need the word to help carry you daily."

"I'll see if I can switch my work schedule so that I can come. I normally work late on Thursdays."

"Okay. Before I go, I want to have a word of prayer with you. Lord, we thank You for this time of sharing. I lift up Sister Brenda to You. Lord, I pray that she rids herself of all of her old emotionally habits and that she doesn't allow the enemy to continue to trick her. Lord, fill her with Your love and give her a new heart to work with. Lord, she needs your love, peace, and joy. Lord, teach her how to speak life into situations that appear to be dead. Lord, release her of the fix it burden that she's carrying and give her relief in You. Oh Lord, wrap her up in your arms and give her the comfort and strength that she needs. Lord, I thank you because I know you're able to turn it around and give her a fresh outlook and a renewed mind. In your mighty name I pray, Amen. Thank you, Lord! Bless Your name. Hallelujah! I believe He's going to do it, Sister Brenda." Ruthie Nell was clapping her hands and praising God.

"Thank you, God! Thank you God," Brenda chimed in.

"That's it. Go on, give Him praise in advance for the victory."

"Sister Sanders, thank you so much for your prayers. When you called me, I was feeling broken and didn't know which way to turn, but now I have a ray of hope thanks to you," Brenda cried.

"No need to thank me. Let's just continue to thank God. He orchestrated this phone call. He knew the outcome beforehand. Tonight rest in His word and you'll sleep like a baby. God bless you, dear, and I hope to see you Thursday night."

"God bless you, too, and I'll try my best to be there."

Brenda hung up the phone and let out a long sigh. Sister Sanders's prayer truly blessed her. She picked up her Bible and began to read it.

Tonight she was going to learn what it meant to rest in the word.

Chapter 8

Willie's phone rang at 6:45 Sunday morning. He opened one eye as he grabbed the phone. Margie Phelps didn't wait for his 'hello'. She started in as soon as he answered, "Willie Jr., I'm sorry but I can't make it to Sunday school this morning. That slipped disc in my back is acting up again. You think you can lead the song and close us out in prayer?"

That would mean he'd actually need to be at church about an hour earlier than he'd planned. Willie rolled his eyes but tried to put a smile in his voice as he answered, "Yes, ma'am. I can do it."

"Thank you."

Willie had expected her to say "good-bye" immediately, but she seemed to be waiting for something. His manners kicked in as he waited for his elder to dismiss him from the conversation. "Is there anything else you need?"

"Willie Lee Jr., I just told you I was sick," she snapped.

And? "Yes, ma'am?"

"Well, if you next in line to be the shepherd of Lee Chapel, you might as well start actin' like it now. When one of your sheep is hurt, you 'posta pray for 'em!" she demanded. "And if I should end up going to emergency, you need to come see about me."

"Oh. Um…" Willie stalled. He wasn't his father.

He wasn't a shepherd. He wasn't a healer. And he sure wasn't one for hanging around sick people. "Well, I will put you on my prayer list."

"On a prayer list?"

"Yes, ma'am."

She tsked. "Lord, Lord, Lord. By the time you get to prayin' for your prayer list, I could be six feet under. Never mind, Willie Jr. I'll pray for myself. Bye."

Willie had raised up in bed and stared at the phone in disbelief as the screen went blank. Despite growing up at Lee Chapel, this was a side of Sister Margie Phelps he had never seen before. *Maybe she should be the next pastor.*

He tried to go back to sleep, but the woman's words rang in his mind: *Well, if you next in line to be the shepherd of Lee Chapel, you might as well start actin' like it now.*

As a preacher's kid, Willie had some idea of how much pressure people might put on men of God. Pastors. On one hand, he liked how people admired and adored his father. People in the community trusted Willie Lee Sr.'s words, actions, and intent. And they had good reason. His father had been in the military, worked hard and retired a civilian job, and founded a church that served its members and the surrounding neighborhood well. He was well-respected and had strong connections in every corner of Pecan Forest— black and white, rich and poor, Christians and unbelievers, too.

In a word, his father had favor.

But Willie Jr. didn't think he had such favor. In fact, he knew he didn't because he was nothing like his father outside of the spotlight. That favor came at a price. Willie couldn't count the number of hours his father spent at the kitchen table with the Bible and a notepad set before him. Or the times he'd walked in on his father praying fervently in the living room calling out people's names before the Lord or asking God for a Word. Sometimes, his father even cried on behalf of someone who was sick or lost. It was painful to watch his father go through such anguish for people that Willie figured probably weren't praying for themselves nearly as hard as their pastor was.

His father could have been a great coach, a public speaker, or a businessman in Dallas or some other big city. But instead, he said he'd followed the Lord's leading and planted a church in Pecan Forest.

Willie Jr. wondered if his life would have been better had his father chosen a different path instead of always trying to do things God's way. It always seemed as though his dad had settled instead of really being somebody.

Maybe I'm settling, too.

When he couldn't get back to sleep, Willie decided he might as well get up and eat breakfast. He grabbed his robe, brushed his teeth, washed his face, and headed to the kitchen. The pathway from the bedroom to the kitchen had somehow become littered with his clothes and shoes and other belongings. Since Brenda left, everything stayed exactly where he put it—on the floor, on the coffee table, or on the couch. He'd never lived in such clutter. Apparently, the women in his life—his mother and Brenda—had been cleaning up after him all his life.

Willie ignored the junk for now and grabbed the box of Honey Nut Cheerios from the top of the refrigerator and a bowl from the cabinet. He noted there were no more clean spoons left after this one when he looked in the utensil drawer.

Next, he poured the milk in the bowl and settled himself at the table. He took a bite of the cereal and immediately spewed it back into the bowl. "Ugh!" The milk was spoiled.

He rushed back to the refrigerator and checked the date it waw two days past the expiration.

Willie could only shake his head. *This wouldn't have happened if Brenda was here.*

He needed his wife back. Like yesterday.

There was a knock at the door. Willie darted to answer it, wondering if perhaps it might be Brenda returning. Answering his fondest wish. He swung the door open and frowned at the sight of his uncle Joseph, dressed and ready for church.

"Don't look so happy to see me," Joseph teased as walked into the apartment, inviting himself inside.

"Morning."

Joseph stood with his hands on his hips and

surveyed the place. "Man, what's going on here? Looks like a pig sty."

"Tell me about it," Willie admitted without telling Joseph that Brenda had left. "We'll get to it."

Joseph put a hand on Willie's shoulder. "Well, since y'all obviously need a maid, I have the solution for you. Misty Blue is racing again next week. People think her winning last week was a fluke. They're all betting against him, but my friend at the track says Misty Blue is stronger than ever. You have to get in on this, Willie. And the more you put down the better. I could almost kick myself for not betting more last week."

"I already put my inheritance in the account," Willie said. "If I withdraw it now, Brenda will think I'm blowing it all, and right now, I don't need her to think any less of me."

"But you're not blowing it. You're *investing* it," Joseph said with pleading eyes.

"I can't," Willie said.

"So…what about option two. The church's money. We discussed it last time and you said you'd think about it."

An uneasy feeling crept into Willie's stomach. "Man, I don't think—"

"No, no no." Joseph looked Willie square in the eyes. "Dude. Your life is terrible. Your father gave his life to the church. Now, if your father wants you to serve these people, it's only fair that you make up for all he did to keep their behinds out of jail, off the streets—he gave thousands of dollars worth of food and toys to the neighborhood hoodrats every year. No disrespect, but the least he could have done was give you more than five thousand dollars every two years."

Up until this morning, Willie might not have given Joseph's words a second thought. But now, after talking to Sister Margie Phelps, he was starting to think the entire church owed the Lee family since his father sacrificed so much for them. *Ungrateful hypocrites.*

Joseph continued, "So if you take a little something from the church, it's not the end of the world. It's payback. Plus, it doesn't really matter anyway because when Misty Blue wins, we'll put it right back in the offering plate. We're just using this money to make money, the way I see it. No harm done."

"I guess—"

"I guess you'd better stop guessing and get moving. The Bible says God helps those who help themselves," Joseph said.

Willie nodded in agreement.

"Great. So here's the plan…"

Joseph went on to describe how he would be standing at the collection plate with Deacon Moody. He would convince Deacon Moody that his hearing aid wasn't working properly by mouthing but not actually speaking any words. Deacon Moody would then think he needed to run home and put on a new hearing aid so he could hear the sermon.

Then Willie was to come in and act like he, too, was speaking so Deacon Moody would be convinced that there was a problem. They would write a note to Deacon Moody telling him that Willie would help count the money, sign off on the deposit slip, and then later deposit the money to the church's account.

A few hours later, the plan was actually working quite well up until Assistant Pastor Grady walked into the office just as Deacon Moody was preparing to leave.

"Excuse me. I left my notes in the top drawer," Grady said.

Deacon Moody's eyebrows shot up. "Hey! I can hear him!"

Willie froze.

Joseph mouthed silent words to Deacon Moody.

Grady asked, "Joseph, did you say something?"

"Mmm hmm." Joseph nodded, causing confusion for Deacon Moody again.

Deacon Moody tapped his hearing aid again. "Naw, I didn't hear what you said just now. Thing must have a short or something."

Grady, too busy to question the scene but feeling perfectly fine that there was nothing wrong so long as Deacon Moody was in the midst of the money situation, left the three men alone again as he returned to the sanctuary.

Willie hadn't been so scared since he was a teenager sneaking back into his bedroom window.

"I guess I'd better head on home and switch out these batteries."

Willie forgot the game and spoke audibly, "Okay."

Joseph kicked Willie's leg under the desk.

"I heard you that time!" Deacon Moody exclaimed.

Willie moved his lips again.

"Shoot. Gone out again," the older man said. "I'll be right back."

And just like that, Willie and Joseph had all they needed to bet on Misty Blue and set things straight for Willie's future.

Chapter 9

Today was the day. Willie and Joseph were planning to bet all $1700 collected in both the Sunday school and the Sunday morning offering. Since the past Sunday had been the first of the month, the total amassed had been much more than usual.

Willie was watching television as he waited for Joseph, but he couldn't focus on the screen. All he could think about was what would happen if they lost. He'd have to pay the money back from what he had left of his five thousand dollars. He had spent five hundred on two pairs of shoes, three hundred on a new water pump for the truck. He'd paid off a few tickets and bought some clothes—a task with Courtney that she was more than willing to help with.

They had driven three hours to Houston the day before, a Friday, and shopped at the kinds of stores Willie normally avoided at an upscale mall with valet parking.

Courtney convinced him that he should "splurge a little," including a $225 dress she wanted in Neiman Marcus. Brenda would never have purchased something so extravagant. So tight. So sexy. He had to admit—the black fabric clung to Courtney in all the right places.

"How do I look?" she had asked when she stepped out of the dressing room and approached him as he sat on a bench waiting outside.

Willie had answered breathlessly, "Amazing."

She twirled around, giving him a full view. "I have to agree. Can I keep it? Pretty please?"

He liked the way she begged. Made him feel like someone actually needed him. "By all means."

"Thank you!" She had hugged him and kissed his cheek.

He nearly drowned in her pool of gratitude— something he never got from Brenda.

Courtney was the kind of woman who could make a man feel like a king.

Willie eagerly paid for the dress and walked out of the store with Courtney clinging to his arm. "Thank you, thank you, thank you, big daddy!"

"Only the best."

Yet even as he said those words, Willie knew all of this was out of his league. But hopefully not for long. Not if Misty Blue came through. This could be his lifestyle.

Except he'd have Brenda instead of Courtney. When Brenda saw that he was adding more money to the account, she'd have more respect for him. She'd put on those sexy nighties again. All would be well.

What *didn't* go well was when Brenda saw the charges to Neiman Marcus on their checking account the next day.

"What's *wrong* with you?" she had fussed. "You've already spent almost a thousand dollars in less than a week!"

Have I?

Rather than argue with him, Brenda had decided to take her name off the account. She wanted nothing else to do with him or his money. "'Cause when you run out, you're not going to be dipping into *my* funds next month trying to pay rent."

A horn blew outside Willie's complex. He knew it had to be Joseph coming to pick him up and take him to the racetrack.

Willie grabbed his keys from the cluttered coffee table and turned off the television with the remote control. He stuffed his feet into his new Nikes and kicked debris out of his path as he walked out the door.

Even as he headed to the track, he prayed silently. *Lord, I know this is wrong. Especially with the church's money. But I'm in a tight spot. I need my wife back. You want marriages to succeed, right? So I need Misty Blue to win. Just this one time. So I can get my life together. And then after I get it together, I'll give it to you probably. Amen.*

"Man, you look like you scared to leave your momma on the first day of kindergarten," Joseph teased as Willie entered his Aunt Galatia's BMW.

He strapped on the seatbelt. "How'd you pry the keys to *this* car out of her fingers?" Willie knew first-hand that his Aunt Galatia loved that vehicle almost more than life itself.

"Your mother and my wife are enjoying their day at

the spa. Your mother drove, so that left me with this ride all to myself." Joseph headed to the highway.

"My aunt will go crazy when she finds out you took her car," Willie warned.

"I ain't scared of my wife," Joseph boasted.

"Yeah, right." Willie had to laugh. Aunt Galatia might have been smitten by Joseph's attention, but she didn't play when it came to her car.

"Well, when I break her off some of this cash we're about to win, she'll stop fussing and start rejoicing," he said.

Joseph informed Willie that today would be Misty Blue's last race for a while. Her owners were so impressed, they were secretly considering moving her to a more competitive league according to Joseph's inside source.

"She must be really fast." Willie hoped as he spoke the comment.

"Faster than anyone thought she'd ever be. You know, they say when she was born, one of her legs was twisted. They had to break it and set it in place. Her nerves on that leg don't work as well. Thought that was gonna be a problem, but all it means now is that she don't feel fatigue in that leg—her *leading* leg. That's why she's so fast. She can't feel tired."

"Mmmm."

"Misty Blue is a sign from God."

Willie doubted that, but he nodded anyway.

"I don't feel no ways tired..." Joseph sang.

Willie gave Joseph the slant-eye, but his Uncle wasn't paying any attention. He was caught up in his own rendition of James Cleveland's song.

"I don't believe He brought Misty this far, to leave her."

Watching his uncle go from conniving gambler to singing deacon in less than sixty seconds made Willie wonder how on earth he had gotten in this situation with Joseph. That uneasy feeling in Willie's gut returned again. He needed to tell Joseph to turn around that very moment and he knew it. But they were already on the highway. He'd already stolen the church's money. He'd already premeditated this much sin. Why stop now when it might pay off?

Seated between Joseph and a man so large with a pair of overalls and beard so long his name had to be "Bubba," Willie waited for the horses' gates to swing open.

They'd watched three races before the one they'd come to see. With each race, Willie's heart pounded faster. Faster. Faster.

What if she loses? But what if she wins?

It was too late now to change his mind. They had already placed their bets with the lady attending their section of the stands. She had a hand-held device—looked almost like credit card processing machines—and she'd taken bets and plenty of cash from the people around them. Willie had listened as much as he could. No one seemed to be betting on Misty Blue. No one except him and Joseph.

When the woman had printed off the receipt and handed it to Joseph, he smacked the paper against his hand and said to Joseph, "The golden ticket."

"It better be."

Now, as the announcer named off the horses and their jockeys, Willie's hands clenched his knee caps. When the gates opened, he stood. Despite cheers from the crowd, the whole world went silent in Willie's ears as he watched Misty Blue's dark brown coat shoot out to the front of the pack.

Yes! Yes!

"Come on, Mistaaaaaay!" Joseph hollered.

Willie balled his fists and mumbled, "Come on, Misty. Come on, girl."

She was doing it! She was winning! The jockey, nearly doubled over, rode her beautifully. They were like a well-oiled machine. A beautiful sight to see.

Willie felt his heart grow jubilant as the horse passed the half-way point around the track, still a head above the second place horse. He jumped from his seat. "Come on, Misty Blue! Come on! Please, God!"

Jockeys seemed to lean lower as the horses came in for the final stretch.

Willie couldn't even watch anymore. He crossed his fingers. Held his breath. The crowd grew louder. *Please, God! Please!*

"Misty Blue takes the win!" the announcer finally blared.

Willie exhaled as stars passed through his vision.

Joseph jumped up and down, pulling Willie into a hug. "I told you! I told you, man! We did it!"

"Thank God," Willie said as he sat down. The adrenaline rush threatened to make him pass out right there in his seat. He was glad this ordeal was over.

But as soon as the attendant returned with the printout showing the amount of $6822.88 for them to claim at the cashout station, the numbers spoke louder than his queasy stomach. *That's almost seven thousand dollars.* After paying back the church's $1700 and paying their informant a tip, he and Joseph were walking away with about $2300 each. For doing *nothing*.

This is free money.

He and Joseph hurried to collect their money. Once back in the car, Joseph counted out the cash in hundred-dollar increments.

Willie had never held so much cash in his hands at one time. Sure, he'd gotten the check from his father, but it had been deposited to a bank. This was cold, hard cash. Felt good in his hands.

Joseph put the key in the car's ignition but didn't turn on the engine. He looked at Willie. "We're on a lucky streak. We can't stop now."

With the smell of fresh money in the car, Willie had to agree.

Chapter 10

The lucky streak continued the next week when they bet on an underrated horse by the name of Sweet Tooth. Willie and Joseph didn't win quite as much because it wasn't the first Sunday. Offering wasn't as large. They should have been in a position to use their own money on the races, but somehow the math wasn't working out.

Both he and Joseph had managed to spend their winnings from Misty Blue's win in less than ten days.

When they cashed out after the second race, Joseph said, "This time, I'm going to make it last."

"Same here," Willie vowed, tucking the $1800 in his pocket as they headed back to the parking lot. He was rich again, and determined not to ever fall back into the pit of being broke in a matter of days.

Joseph pushed a homemade copy of the Williams Brothers' greatest hits into the CD player and began singing along with the gospel music as they left the race rack. He sung along, "Jesus…will never…say no."

Willie listened as Joseph emphasized the lyrics he obviously wanted to believe.

This isn't right. Maybe Joseph genuinely thought it was okay to live a double-life, but Willie knew better. He could almost hear his father's warnings. His preachings. His teachings about how important it was to practice what you preach.

That's exactly why I'm not preaching, Willie thought. He could never live up to Willie Sr.'s example. He didn't have the patience with people. He had no desire to read the Bible. Shoot, he didn't even have a first lady anymore.

Joseph pulled into Willie's apartment complex and parked. "We on for next Saturday?"

"I don't know, Joseph. Maybe we could skip a week. Don't want to press our luck, you know?" Willie unlocked his door and reached for the handle to get out of the car.

Joseph quickly locked the doors again from the driver's console. "No! We gotta strike while the iron is hot! If we keep this up, we won't ever have to work again. Long as my friend keeps giving us the heads-up. All it takes is one big one."

"It's just—"

"Willie. Have *faith.*"

"Huh?"

"Faith and works, because faith without works is dead," Joseph said.

The way Joseph used scriptures to justify his own agenda rubbed Willie the wrong way. "Man, if we're going to do wrong, let's just be wrong. Don't try to make it right."

"Whatever you say, preacher's kid." Joseph laughed. "All I know is, we're on a roll. You'd be a fool *and* a hypocrite to quit now."

That last accusation bit into Willie's conscience.

Being a hypocrite had always been one of his greatest fears. And yet, that's exactly what he was becoming.

"Just one more time, Willie. I'll leave you alone after that. The next race is even bigger. Mo' money, mo' money, mo' money. Enough to set us for at least the next six months—give me more than enough money to bet in the future. I'll find me another business partner. Plus, that'll leave you about four months to get all sanctified so you can move on to your next hustle as pastor of Lee Chapel."

Willie wished he could say something in his defense, but with the money burning in his pocket, how could he defend himself? "One more, Joseph—that's it. I'm out."

"Not a problem." Joseph unlocked the doors and let Willie out. "Talk to you later."

"Yeah." Willie got out of the car and shut the door behind him.

Apart from Joseph's presence, guilt seemed to sink into Willie's heart. *This is crazy.* So crazy, in fact, that he suddenly became hungry. He didn't even go inside the messy apartment and try to cook something in the stained, crust pots and pans. He headed to McDonald's instead, contemplating the situation along the way.

Would Joseph ever stop gambling? Did Grady Sanders reconcile the checking statements at the end of the month? Would he question why it took so long for the deposits to be made to the church's account? How long could they play the trick on Deacon Moody?

And what about Brenda? She'd been ignoring his phone calls and messages, and Willie was tired of chasing her. If she didn't want him, Courtney sure did.

Willie thought about giving a tithe and offerings from his winnings, but he wasn't sure if the Lord liked dirty money. He decided instead to donate to a young Pop Warner cheerleading squad selling cookies in front of McDonalds. Hopefully, it would do some good.

As he folded the twenty dollar bill so that it could fit into the slot on top of the collection box, he smiled at the little girl with two pigtails and a snaggle-toothed grin.

"Thank you, Mister," she said.

"You're welcome."

The innocence of her gratitude made Willie wonder when his own innocence had ceased to exist. *How did I become a man who gambles with the church's money?*

Willie made the decision that he would definitely be "out" of the gambling game after this last time. It was too hard living with these condemning thoughts. If he kept this up, he'd probably get sick or start having nightmares and go crazy. He might not ever live up to his father's dreams, but he couldn't live in this gutter. *Maybe Joseph can do it, but I can't.*

Until then, Willie had one more week left to live like a double-minded heathen.

Courtney parked her car next to the shopping cart bin at Walmart and rushed to the passenger side of the Mercedes Willie had rented for their weekend excursion.

"Oooh!" She squealed as she fastened her seatbelt. "A Mercedes Benz! You really came up with your father's will, huh?" She gave him a smack on his cheek and then threw her bag in the back seat.

Willie Jr. decided not to tell her that he didn't actually own the vehicle. "Nothing but the best for you."

Courtney breathed in deeply. "Real leather seats. I love it!"

Watching her smile, seeing her pleased because of something he'd done was almost worth the grim sliding across his heart. Sneaking around wasn't his style. But somebody was obviously running their mouth and telling Brenda that Willie was seeing someone.

Even his mother had called and asked, "Son, are you fooling around on your wife?"

"My *estranged* wife," he clarified. He was certain that Joseph must have said something to Aunt Galatia, and Aunt Galatia had relayed the message to his mother that either Brenda Lee was gone or she'd stopped her housekeeping responsibilities.

"Brenda ain't estranged, unless you're doing something strange. Now what's going on, Willie Michael Lee, Jr.?"

When his mother pulled the whole-name card, there

was no easy way of skirting past her question. "Momma, you and Daddy taught me not to involve other people in my marital affairs. Right?"

"Yes, but we never told you to go out and *have* an affair." She had turned it around.

"Momma, I'm not having an affair," Willie Jr. said. Then he had hurried off the phone.

He'd never been in the habit of lying to his mother. Technically, he hadn't lied. He wasn't having an affair with Courtney because they hadn't slept together because, by Willie's definition, it's not an affair until two people sleep together.

So far all they had done was shop, dine, and give each other a few pecks.

However, this weekend might change everything. He and Courtney were going to Choctaw Casino in Oklahoma City for an overnight getaway. Not so much to get away from Pecan Forest, but to get away from nosy folks who assumed he and Courtney had already become lovers.

The trip was a three-hour drive. Willie was prepared to pay for two hotel rooms. But he wasn't sure if Courtney would request her own room. They hadn't discussed the details.

"I am sooooo glad to be with you this weekend." She chirped, grabbing his hand across the wood grain console. "You make me the happiest girl in the world."

Willie's chest puffed up, straining against his seat belt. He did his best imitation of J.J. from Good Times.

"Well…ur…uh…what can I say?" He stroked his chin, waiting for Courtney to laugh.

She gave him a quizzical look.

"It's J.J. from Good Times," Willie said.

"Oh. That was one of those old TV shows, right?" Courtney said.

Willie's lungs deflated. "Yeah." Reminders about fifteen years between them always seemed to pop up out of nowhere. Courtney was young enough to have been his high school accident.

She stroked the back of his neck. "But you're not old, Schnookums. You're perfect for me. Oh, but there's something I need to tell you."

"What?"

"I really couldn't find anything really nice to wear tonight. Can we go shopping? Please? I want to make you look like the luckiest man in the entire casino tonight."

And that she did. Courtney bought a tight, white dress with keyholes along the side from her waist all the way down to the slit at her knee. Her long, shapely legs peeked out with every step, giving every man a taste of what they couldn't have. She swept her hair up in a loose bun and donned the Swarovski crystal earrings he'd purchased in addition to the dress and heels at one of the shops inside the casino.

Courtney looked like a million bucks—partly because Willie felt like that's how much he had spent. But it was worth every penny to see other men nodding at him, almost congratulating him silently for catching such a beautiful woman. The admiring glances made Willie feel almost like he'd felt when he was in high school walking down the halls of Pecan Forest High School. Nerds stepped aside. Unpopular nobodies quieted their conversations when he and other football players came close. They were envied and adored. They were *somebody*.

The feeling was priceless. He could get used to being with Courtney all the time.

He and Courtney checked into a single hotel room, grabbed a bite to eat, then spent some time at the machines. Willie quickly won three hundred dollars but lost four hundred and twenty. Courtney was up, though. She won fifty from the two hundred Willie had given her to spend.

She cashed in her winnings and bought a purse at another casino shop with her money.

Determined to at least break even, Willie declined to come to the room with her when she asked. He was busy betting and pushing buttons.

"Well, at least give me the key," she said seductively, "so I can…get ready for you."

He raised an eyebrow.

Courtney bit the nail of her index finger.

Willie gave her the key card.

She bent down and whispered in his ear, "I'll be waiting for you."

Willie noticed how her cleavage spilled over the top

of the dress's low neckline. "O…okay."

Courtney swished away. Willie watched as several sets of eyes followed her Coke-bottle figure walk toward the elevators.

"Can I get you something to drink?" a waitress asked.

"Yeah. Crown on the rocks," Willie stated quickly. The thought of being with another woman required a drink indeed.

Am I really going through with this?

For all the things he'd done wrong in his marriage, he had done one thing right: He had never cheated on Brenda.

Am I cheating?

His body said no, but his conscience said yes. And he could all but hear his father saying, "Yes, son. You're still married. Don't do this to Brenda."

Willie kept playing the machine. Waiting for a jackpot. Hoping his machine would soon be the one with bells and whistles chiming madly.

"Here you go, hun," the waitress returned with his drink. Willie downed it quickly.

Five minutes later, he ordered another. Then he had a Pina Colada. And a margarita. Whatever he had after that, Willie couldn't remember.

At some point, he lost all the money he'd earmarked for gambling and then some. He somehow made his way to his hotel room. And that was all he could remember.

The next morning, he woke, sitting up in the chair in the hotel room. Fully clothed in the same attire he'd worn the night before. His dry mouth tasted like fifty rotten, rancid eggs—a gross yet familiar taste. He must have vomited somewhere at some time.

Courtney lay asleep in bed, under the covers. *Is she wearing anything? Did we have sex?*

He didn't wait to find out.

Willie grabbed his bag and locked himself in the restroom. He brushed his teeth and rinsed his mouth until the taste of bile disappeared. He showered and changed into a second outfit.

Courtney's knock at the door startled him. "Babe, let me in. I have to use the restroom."

"Just a second."

Babe? She'd never called him that before. *Maybe we did do something.*

He opened the door and sighed with relief to see Courtney dressed in pajamas. "Good morning."

"Good morning," she said. She hugged him.

Willie froze in place, afraid of what might be happening and what might have already happened.

Courtney looked up at him. She gave him a girly smile. "Okay. You can get out now."

She didn't want him to see her undress. That was a good sign. "Um…Courtney…we didn't…do anything last night, did we?"

She rolled her lips between her teeth and sighed. "We weren't…*able* to do anything last night."

He squinted at her.

"You were drunk. I tried to get you to lie down in bed with me, but you insisted on the chair. Then you ran to the bathroom. You threw up and passed out."

"Oh." Willie hid his joy with a simple response.

"But don't worry," Courtney chirped up, "all of my friends who date older guys say it's normal for…a man your age…to have problems. You can go see a doctor and—"

"Wait," he stopped her, "you and your friends make a habit of dating men old enough to be your father?"

She shrugged. "It's all good. I mean, we're all just having a good time. No harm, no foul. Right?"

He nodded, though in his heart Willie knew this whole situation was foul.

The last horse race couldn't get here soon enough.

Chapter 11

"Galatia, baby, I'm sorry it took me so long to get home last night. Junior called and said he needed me to help him with something."

"Help him with what?" she fussed.

After leaving the track yesterday, Joseph had convinced Willie that they should get in on a dice game. Joseph had won $1000 but because of his greed he'd lost it back. He now only hand a measly $5 to his name. He and Willie had spent several hours drinking and waddling in self-pity.

"Man stuff. Baby come here. Don't you believe me?" He wooed her and pulled her into his arms.

"You know you look sexy when you mad. Give me some of that sweet sweet."

Joseph caressed her and gave her a long, passionate kiss.

Galatia was melting by his touch until the buzzing sound of his cell phone interrupted them.

"Give me one minute. I'll be right back." Joseph retrieved his phone and left the room.

He entered the bathroom to answer the call.

"Man, what are we going to do?" Willie Jr. shouted before he could say hello.

"Calm down. Imma think of something."

"I knew I shoulda went with my first mind. Now I gotta pay the church back. Brenda won't even talk to me," Willie shouted.

"Why you yelling at me? You wanted in. You could have told me no, so don't try to act like this is all my fault." Joseph back peddled.

"Unbelievable, just freaking unbelievable/ I can't believe you right now."

"Answer this, do I have access to the church's money? No. Do I have access to your money? No. Did I hold a gun to your head and make you place that bet? No."

"It was your idea," Willie said, getting more irritated.

"I never said you had to do it. I just presented it to you," Joseph pointed out.

"Yeah, you presented it as a sure thing and I took the bait. Just like Eve in the garden, I let the serpent deceive me. My father was right when he told me to stay away from you. I should have listened to him." Willie hung up the phone before Joseph could reply.

Joseph suddenly felt nervous. He didn't know what Willie planned on doing. What if he told Ephesia, or better yet, what if he told Grady Sanders? Joseph hadn't planned on going to church today but felt like he needed to be there just in case Willie decided to run his mouth.

When Joseph entered the bedroom, Galatia had his blue and grey pinstriped suit on the bed. She was wearing a blue and grey dress to match with a big blue hat. Galatia loved to dress like her husband. All of the ladies at the church glared at them every Sunday and Galatia loved the attention.

"Honey, hurry up and get dressed so we can go," Galatia stated as she was in the closet looking for her shoes. "Who was that on the phone?"

"That was Junior calling to ask if I was going to church today," he lied.

"Why wouldn't you be going to church? And why on earth would he be calling to ask that?" she questioned.

"I guess he's taking his new role seriously now, since I'm a Deacon and he's the Pastor. Guess he wants to make sure I'm there for Sunday service," he embellished.

"Well, he got some nerves thinking he should check up on you. Somebody needs to check up on *him*." She rolled her eyes as she walked across the room to retrieve her jewelry.

"I don't think he meant it in a bad way," Joseph replied.

He didn't want Galatia to be in an uproar because she would certainly let loose on Willie Jr. and anybody else who got in her way.

"Let me get dressed so that we can go to breakfast before church. Girl, you wearing that dress." He kissed her forehead.

Joseph and Galatia made their way to the LaQuinta Inn and Suites to eat breakfast. Joseph had convinced her that there was nothing wrong with them eating there. He'd told her that the food was free. Galatia knew the food was free to guests of the hotel but didn't argue with Joseph. She often worried about them getting caught but today when she spotted a group of people who looked like they were in town for a conference, her fears disappeared.

"These waffles and eggs are hitting the spot. Umm umm, they good," Joseph said as he smacked.

"I'm glad it's crowded in here, so we won't get questioned."

"You worry too much. I been doing this for years. You ain't got nothing to worry about."

"Joseph, I need to ask you something and I want you to tell me the truth."

"Aww man, here we go. What is it?" he said, dropping his fork.

"What did you and Junior do? And before you prepare a big elaborate lie, I want you to know I overheard your phone conversation."

Joseph's eyes got as big as the waffles he was eating. He thought he had closed the door behind him.

"I want the truth, Joseph," Galatia said sternly.

"It wasn't my fault. Junior gambled away most of his money and the church's offering." He spilled his guts.

"Did I just hear you say he gambled with the

church's money?" she said.

"Yeah, baby. He got the offering, bet on a horse, and lost."

"I can't wait to get to church to let ole wide-necked Grady Sanders know what's been going on," Galatia gloated.

"Whoa whoa. You can't do that?" Joseph said in a panic.

"And why not?"

"Because I was with him. I drove him there and you know they'll try to find a way to put this all on me."

"They can't put this on you. You're not the one who took the church's money, are you?" she asked.

Joseph hesitated before he answered her. If he told her no, Willie Jr. would surely tell the church how he helped get the offering from Deacon Moody. If he told her yes, he didn't know what Galatia would do. He decided either way, the outcome wouldn't be good.

"Technically no."

"What do you mean technically?"

"See, what had happened was I was helping with the offering and the batteries in Deacon Moody's hearing aid went dead. He left and when he left Junior took the money," Joseph said, giving her the watered down truth.

"So, you didn't take the money. Willie took the money and that clears you." She smiled.

"The church won't see it that way. They'll want to know why I didn't say something or do something to try to stop him, especially since I'm a Deacon," Joseph pointed out.

"Willie is a grown man who made a decision to steal money from the church. The church where I pay my tithes and offering to. The church that his father founded, and he ain't got the sense of a baboon. Willie Sr. is probably rolling over in his grave behind this. That's why I got to let the church know before things get worse," Galatia ranted.

"Galatia, baby, let me handle this. I'll help get Junior out of this mess," Joseph offered.

"Help him how?"

"I don't know, but give me some time to think of something. What does the Bible say—love covers a multitude of sins."

"There's a difference between covering and covering up. I'm going to the board today so that this can be taken care of now. Willie Jr. needs help. Once a thief, always a thief, and you know that old saying, if you cheat, you lie, if you lie, you steal, if you steal, you kill. I don't want nobody to end up dead."

"Galatia, you getting yourself all worked up for nothing. You know Junior ain't no killer."

"How I know? I didn't think he would steal but he did," she pointed out.

"How do you think this is going to make Ephesia feel? I mean, she just lost her husband and that's got to be rough on her," Joseph said as if he was really concerned about Ephesia, although he knew his sister-in-law couldn't stand him and the feeling was mutual.

"Ephesia will be just fine. I think God is allowing all of this to happen so that my sister can finally see her precious, sweet Willie Jr. for who He really is. In her eyes Junior is perfect and can do no wrong. Well today she's going to hear the truth, and once the truth is out they'll have no choice but to let you be the next Pastor of Lee Chapel," Galatia said proudly.

"I'm a Deacon not a Pastor or preacher. I don't know nothing about preaching."

"That's okay, you know the Bible enough for them to turn the church over to you. Grady's getting old, so with you being young you'll get voted in. You know all of those old biddies will vote for you."

"Galatia, baby, I'm not qualified to be a Pastor. You didn't even ask me if it was something I wanted to do. I'm not interested in preaching at all."

"Willie ain't qualified either, so that makes two of you. Now let's go before we be late," Galatia said as she gathered her things and headed towards the hotel's exit.

Chapter 12

"Galatia, baby listen to me. I don't think it's a good idea to try to out Junior."

"I'm going to Grady as soon as we arrive and tell him everything I know. It's time for things to be put into their proper place. We won't be playing seconds to nobody no more. It's time for us to get the respect we deserve, and I can't wait to see the look on my sister's face," she said with a wicked look.

Joseph side eyed Galatia and at that moment he realized that this was deeper than what he thought. Clearly Galatia wanted to throw Willie's indiscretions in Ephesia's face. He couldn't believe that she was really willing to purposely hurt her sister.

"Why are you so against Ephesia?" he inquired.

"You sound silly. I'm not against my sister," Galatia uttered.

"Sounds like you're ready to rub this in her face."

"It's not rubbing it in her face, it's called telling the truth. The Bible says the truth will set you free."

By the look on Galatia's face Joseph knew there was nothing he could say or do to convince her to change her mind.

"There's a way to do everything so just promise me that you will at least wait until after the service before telling anyone."

Joseph pulled into the church parking lot and before

he could turn the engine off, Galatia hopped out of the car. He hoped that she wouldn't tell anyone about the money but knew that she would. For the first time in his life, he was actually nervous. The first thing he thought about doing was leaving, but where would he go. He didn't have any family or friends he could turn to because he burnt all of those bridges.

Oh well, here goes nothing. He sighed as he went into the church.

When Joseph walked into the sanctuary all of the Deacons were lined up ready to start devotion. Galatia was sitting on the second pew with the rest of the Deaconess.

Joseph was about to sit down but Deacon Moody beckoned for him to join them.

Reluctantly he joined them. He was guilty ridden and felt as if the whole congregation was staring at him.

Shine on me, shine on me

Deacon Moody sang

Let the light from the lighthouse

Yes, yes shine on me. Ephesia sang standing to her feet.

"Have your way in this place," Galatia added.

Joseph held his head down while the members of Lee Chapel continued to worship God.

After devotion Pastor Grady Sanders and Willie Jr. walked in.

Willie looked like he'd been up all night. His eyes were blood shot red and his clothes were wrinkled.

Willie didn't wear a suit; he had on black slacks, a black and white button down shirt, with a pair of loafers.

Joseph tried to make eye contact with him but Willie turned his head.

The choir gave their A & B selections and Pastor Sanders got up to preach.

"This morning, my brothers and sisters, I want to preach from a familiar passage of scripture. If you have your Bible please turn to Matthew 16:26. Please stand for the reading of the word. "And it reads: *For what is a man profited, if he shall gain the whole world, and lose his own soul? or what shall a man give in exchange for his soul?*

"My subject today is: Is It Worth It?"

"Alright Pastor, that's a good title," one of the ushers said.

Both Willie and Joseph looked as if they were about to pass out.

Joseph tried to read Willie's face but all he saw was that Willie was sweating.

"I won't be before you long today. I'm not going to try to shout at you. I wanna help some people this morning. Is that alright?"

"That's alright; take your time," Ruthie Nell said.

"The world has so much to offer. It offers things that are appealing to the eyes, but everything that look good ain't good for you."

"You on it," Deacon Moody said.

"The attraction of this world can get you caught up in a heap of trouble. Let's look at the scripture and look at the word gain. To gain means to acquire something, become greater. Stay with me, I'm going somewhere with this. To lose means the exact opposite. It means to have something taken away. Is gaining things more important and more valuable than having a relationship with God? Is it worth it?"

"Not at all," Galatia shouted.

"Church, when you gain things and put them before God, you lose. When your earthly desires become more important than your walk with the Lord, you in big trouble. You headed downhill quick. These old earthly treasures will pass away, so ask yourself, is it worth it? Is it worth you missing eternity with the Lord? Is it worth you losing your soul?"

"My God, my God, you preaching today," Ephesia said.

"I don't know about you but my soul love Jesus and that's why I bless His name. The world didn't die for me, He did. The world can't keep my mind regulated; the world can't answer my prayers; the world can't save me, and the world didn't give me the Holy Ghost."

"Hallelujah! Thank you, Jesus," one of the choir members said.

"Lord you're worthy," Deacon Griffin added.

"I know some of y'all thinking that gaining the world can be beneficial, but don't be fooled. There's a price to pay. I know a man who hit the jackpot, won millions of dollars, but he paid a price. That price was his life. He was hooked on drugs and died from an overdose. You see, what he thought was his gain was actually his loss. The world gives a temporary satisfaction; the only thing that has a lasting satisfaction is Christ. Life in Christ. Seek Him first and all the other things will be added unto you. That's His word and His promise when you meet those conditions."

As Pastor Sanders expounded on the rest of his sermon, Joseph watched Willie. Willie looked distraught. Joseph didn't know if Willie had told Pastor Sanders what happened or if his sermon was just a coincidence.

Finally church was over and Joseph rushed over to talk to Willie. He needed to know what his mindset was.

"Say man, let me holla at you for a minute."

"Holla at me for what? I really don't wanna deal with you no more, man," Willie said and walked off.

Joseph was walking behind him as Galatia rushed to the pulpit area where Pastor Sanders and Deacon Moody were conversing.

"Excuse me, Pastor Sanders. I have some important information I need to share with you and my sister," Galatia said.

"Ephesia and Willie Jr. please meet me up front," Pastor Sanders announced on the microphone.

Joseph tried to make a beeline through the side door but Galatia spotted him and motioned for him to join her.

"What is this about, Sis. Galatia?"

"Pastor Sanders, I know my brother-in-law had a will with specific instructions about the ongoing of the church but after today I'm sure we'll need to do something different," Galatia said, getting to the point.

"What on earth are you talking about?" Ephesia inquired.

"I'm talking about Willie Jr. stealing the church's money."

"Sis. Galatia, I can't allow you to accuse Willie Jr. of something he didn't do," Pastor Sanders cautioned.

"He did it, and I know he did it because Joseph saw him do it," Galatia said.

"That's enough, Galatia. Just stop with your lies. If anything Junior stopped Joseph from stealing the money," Ephesia spat.

"Ladies, ladies, ladies, let's not forget where we are. Now both men are here and neither one of them have said a word, so let's hear from them. I'll start with you, Willie Jr. What happened?" Pastor Sanders said.

Willie looked at his mother and back at Pastor Sanders. He knew there was no way he could lie his way out of this.

"It's the truth, but it was an accident."

"See, I toldya." Galatia gloated.

"An accident? How was it an accident?" Ephesia questioned, looking confused.

"Joseph came to me with a sure way to win some

money. I was desperate to make a come up because I didn't want to wait on my money. We took the money that day when Deacon Moody left and used it at the races. We thought we could get ahead, but as it turns out, we were wrong." Willie said and dropped his head.

"Ain't no need of you being shame now. You wasn't shame when you was betting on that horse," Galatia said.

"Joseph, you are just as responsible as Willie is," Ephesia added.

"Oh no, don't try to drag my husband into this mess." Galatia said, defending Joseph.

"Your husband is the one who gave him the idea," Ephesia interjected.

"She's right, Joseph. As a Deacon you had no business suggesting that Willie take money from the church and you certainly had no business watching him take the money. You're just as guilty as he is." Pastor Sanders stared at Joseph with disbelief.

"He's a grown man, and more than capable of making his own decisions." Joseph chimed in.

"That's right and I think as acting Pastor you should have Willie Sr.'s. will overturned. We don't need a thief trying to lead this flock," Galatia added.

"Sis. Galatia, I suggest you take a long look in the mirror at yourself and stop pointing fingers at others. I know you think you have it all together but you don't. My niece Laverne works at the LaQuinta and says she sees you there quite often eating breakfast. I know you're not staying there so that means you're stealing their breakfast, so sweep around your own front door. A sin is a sin is a sin so you're just as guilty as Willie and Joseph."

Galatia opened her mouth as if she wanted to speak but changed her mind. She was too embarrassed.

"Willie and Joseph, I'm sitting you both down effectively immediately. Willie, I will put you on a payment plan to pay the money back and I want to see both of you at Bible study every Wednesday night. Willie, this church and what it stands for meant a lot to your father and I pray that you'll do some real soul searching and find yourself, son. Ask yourself is it worth it," Pastor Sanders said and left.

Ephesia followed behind him, she was too upset to deal with Willie.

Galatia and Joseph left, too, leaving Willie sitting on the pew.

"No, it's not worth it," he whispered through the tears that were streaming down his face.

He'd lost—lost his dad, lost his wife, lost his mother's respect, and all he'd gained was disappointment.

Chapter 13

The alarm clock screeched Willie out of a sound sleep. He'd been asleep for most of the day. Pastor Grady expected Willie to be at church in an hour for Bible study, followed by service. Willie's church attendance was mandatory. If he didn't attend, Grady would call the police and have him arrested and prosecuted for theft from a non-profit organization.

Since Sunday, Willie had done his best to stay in bed, keep the rooms dark, and close his eyes and his mind to the problems. If he hadn't slept, he probably would have been drinking in order to escape the guilt and the sting in his heart from hurting so many people.

The only reason he wasn't drinking was because he hardly had enough money to buy what he needed to knock himself out for a few days.

Maybe I should start doing drugs.

The very thought startled Willie. He'd done a lot of wild and crazy things and been to his fair share of parties, but the idea of getting high on drugs was so foreign to his thought process, he knew this thought wasn't his own.

Willie shook his head and said out loud, "No." This wasn't him. Stealing thousands of dollars, gambling, lying to his mother, cheating on his wife—none of this was him.

Who is it, then?

The voice in his head was so clear, so strong. It almost scared Willie.

"No!" He yelled loud enough for himself and the voice to hear. *Am I going crazy? Am I possessed?*

Willie quickly jumped out of bed, showered, and prepared himself for church. He arrived at Lee Chapel fifteen minutes early, knowing that Pastor Grady would probably be in the office reviewing his sermon notes.

For the first time since he could remember, Willie had to knock on the back door of the church because he no longer had a key to the church his own father had founded. Again, remorse flooded through his body.

Heavy footsteps approached the door from the other side. "Who is it?"

"It's me. Willie Jr."

The door opened. "What you need, Willie?" Pastor Sanders asked.

"I'd like to come in."

"We don't start until six," he said.

"I know," Willie Jr. said. "I need to talk to you."

Pastor Sanders eyebrow lifted. "How do I know I can trust you, Willie Jr.? How do I know you and Joseph aren't planning to ambush me and rob me so you can make another run at the race track?"

Willie bowed his head. "I guess you don't." Was this what it had come to? No one trusted him, not even his deceased father's best friend?

"Well," Pastor Sanders hesitated. "Come on in. I trust the Lord to protect me from all harm and danger."

"Thank you." Willie followed Grady back to the office where the gambling transgression had been conceived. Willie felt like scrubbing the table, the walls, the floors clean with his hands and a toothbrush. He would spend hours to erase what happened if he could.

He and Grady sat at the desk, his father's Bible open right next to Grady's.

"What did you want to talk to me about?" Grady asked.

Willie sighed. "I heard a voice."

"A voice?"

"Yeah. In my head," Willie said. "I mean, it was like an idea that I never had before. To start doing drugs to help me through this."

"Willie Jr., I'm going to tell you like Jesus told Peter. The enemy wants to sift you like wheat, but I'm praying that your faith fail you not and that when this is all over, you will be used by God to build His Kingdom. Just like the Lord told your father way back when you were a boy."

"So you're praying for me?" Willie Jr. asked.

"Sure am."

"Then why do I feel like it's time for me to start using drugs?"

"Because you've let the enemy talk you out of your destiny and into foolishness for a long time," Grady said. "I have no doubt in my mind that the gambling was Joseph's idea. But you allowed him to persuade you against what you truly believe."

Willie confessed, "That wasn't the first time I stole. I took a little money here and there. I always put it back. I know that doesn't make it right...I just wanted to let you know."

"Well, that was the open door," Grady said. "And Joseph—"

Willie stated adamantly, "I'm done dealing with him."

"I know you are. And the enemy knows it, too. So now he's coming directly to you. He does a really good job of speaking to us and disguising his voice as our own. That's how he does it. If you listen to him about the drugs, you'll listen to him about taking more drugs, becoming violent...eventually, he will try to take your life. Make no mistake—he's not here to play pity-pat with you. He's here to kill, steal, and destroy. He wants you dead, Willie Jr., one way or another."

Willie Jr. shook his head. "I don't want to die."

"Then choose life," Grady said. "Stop running from the only One who can set you free from the power of sin and give you His life, Jesus Christ."

Willie Jr. buried his face in his hands. "You sound just like my father." His voice broke with emotion. Instantly, he found himself crying the way he almost did at his father's funeral. Fatherless, alone, without a covering.

He felt Grady's hands around his shoulder. "Go on and let it out, Willie Jr. You're at a crossroad in your life. It's time to choose."

"I choose Jesus as my savior," Willie said, drying his eyes.

Grady squared up. "Now, are you choosing Him because you're sad about your father's death or because you really want to live your life in such a way that it honors the Lord? So you can hold your head up because He lives in you?"

"I want to be free," Willie Jr. said, "and I want to live right."

Grady's lips formed the widest grin Willie Jr. had ever seen. "Welcome to the family of Christ, Willie Jr. I'm sure your father and all the angels in heaven are rejoicing right now."

Willie fell into Grady's hug. "Thank you." He only wished he had done this sooner.

That evening, when Grady took the pulpit to preach, he seemed to be peeking over at Willie Jr. and smiling every minute or so. Maybe he had always done that. Willie Jr. didn't mind, though. He was ready for this change.

So ready that he hadn't even seen Courtney when she walked into the church. But as soon as Grady dismissed the congregation, Willie found himself looking down at the exposed space in her cleavage. She had been waiting for him at his truck.

"Hi, Willie," she whispered as he tried to unlock the door.

"Hi."

"Haven't heard from you in a few days," she said.

"I've been going through some things," he told her. He unlocked the door, hoping she would step aside.

She bucked her eyes. "Ummm...can we meet somewhere? So we can talk?"

Since he had parked at the back doors of the church, they had a little privacy—enough for him to let her go with some dignity. "Look, Courtney, I...I've made some changes in my life, all right? I'm moving on. Trying to do what God would have me to do."

"Me, too," she claimed. "I thought about what I said to you at the hotel. And I have something to tell you. At first, I was only with you because I thought you had some money. But now I'm thinking that I really like your company. You're a decent guy. You never tried to take advantage of me. There aren't many men like you out there, Willie. I'd like to get to know you. Not just for your money—but as a person. And since we haven't slept together, it shouldn't be too hard to start over. Right? And we can ask God to help us get to know each other the right way."

Willie Jr. stopped. "Courtney, you know I'm married, correct?"

"Yeah, but you obviously don't love her anymore. All you need to do is get a divorce." She shrugged as though marriages came and went as easily as new cell phones.

"It's not that simple."

"No it's not. You don't love her, so—"

"I never told you I didn't love my wife."

"Oh." Courtney's face hardened. "Then I guess you played me as much as I tried to play you, huh?"

"I wasn't playing. I was…I was wrong. And I'm sorry if I hurt you."

Courtney laughed. "And I thought you were different."

"Actually, I am different now. Much different than I was just a few hours ago."

She smacked. "No one changes *that* fast."

Willie tilted his head. "Well, I haven't arrived. But I *have* left. Goodbye, Courtney. I do hope you'll pursue a relationship with the Lord even though there won't be one between me and you."

She crossed her arms. "Wait a minute. Are you trying to get all holy on me, 'cause you sure sounded like a preacher just now."

"You said it," Willie confirmed. "Have a blessed life, Courtney. I have to go."

Chapter 14

Joseph's heart beat wildly as he watched the dice roll and spin to a stop. *Three. No!* A string of cusswords spewed from his lips as the group of men crouched on the concrete around him laughed and collected their gain.

Joseph had lost again. The lucky streak was definitely over. Since Willie Jr. gave up his role as Joseph's gambling partner, Joseph had done nothing but lose. He lost money on the next two horse races, a roll of lottery tickets, a pool match, and now another round of dice.

He was broke. Busted. Even worse, he owed Big Ray $4000. Joseph had been counting on shooting craps—something he'd done successfully since he was a teenager—to put him in a position to at least pay part of the money he owed Big Ray.

Joseph rose, his knees popping. "Naw. I'm out."

Snootie laughed. "Look to me like you ain't got no choice!"

The fellows chimed in, "Worst luck I ever saw," and "Must have broken a mirror or walked under a ladder or something."

"Forget y'all," Joseph said, kicking Drunk Mike's foot out of the way.

Mike stirred but didn't get up off the ground.

"Hey! Leave Drunk Mike alone!" Snootie hollered.

"Ain't his fault you got black cats crossing your path!" Again, the men laughed at Joseph as he walked away. He shoved his hands into the empty pockets of his blue jeans. A chill wind met him as he exited the alley behind the barber shop. *What am I going to do now?* Big Ray would want his money tonight, as they had agreed. The hundred dollars would have been enough to hold him off for the weekend, or until Ephesia got her check at the first of the month.

But now, he had nothing to give Big Ray.

Where can I go? Pecan Forest wasn't big enough for him to hide.

Joseph pulled his starched collar up over his ears, hoping to make it back home without running into Big Ray. This part of town—with hole-in-the-wall stores, clubs, and places to get a stiff drink—was Big Ray's territory. But he wouldn't hesitate to come to Joseph's house to collect, if need be.

Joseph stopped at the end of the block and hugged the side of Sugar's Bar-B-Que shack. He peeked around the bricks to see if Big Ray was anywhere in sight on the next street over. He breathed a sigh of relief when he saw that the street was clear.

But that relief was short-lived.

"You got my money?" Big Ray's voice came from behind.

Willie watched with both delight and humility as

111

Sugar counted Willie's hard-earned money into his hand. "Twenty, forty, sixty, eighty, one, and two."

The short stack of bills seemed like nothing compared to the last time Joseph slapped hundreds of dollars into Willie's hands.

And yet, this money—this clean money—felt heavier. Cleaner. Better. It was a start to paying back what he owed the church. "Thank you, Sugar."

Miss Sugar, at almost seventy years old, had watched almost everyone in Pecan Forest grow up. She gave Willie a wrinkled smile. "Your daddy was a good man, Willie, Jr. And the good book says if a child is raised up right, when he's old, he won't depart from it. That's the only reason I'm giving you a chance at my store. 'Cause I know your daddy raised you up right." She slammed the cash register shut. "But I heard what you did with the church's money. If I find out you stealin' from me, the scripture ain't gon' come true for you 'cause you won't have a chance to get old before I make you depart this life, you hear?"

"Yes, ma'am."

Willie Jr. knew she was telling the truth, too. Sugar did a little time for shooting at her third husband's mistress. Probably wouldn't make her any difference to do a few more years if she felt someone wronged her bad enough.

"I'm keeping track of your money, too," Sugar told him. "So you can pay taxes and everything."

"Yes, ma'am."

Willie Jr. folded the money, put it in his wallet, and then put the wallet in his pocket underneath his apron. He returned to the kitchen and began running hot water, preparing for the next batch of dishes that was surely soon to come.

Washing dishes at Sugar's Bar-B-Que shack wasn't exactly what Willie Jr. thought he'd be doing at this point in his life, but it was turning out to be almost therapeutic. Dunking each mountain of dirty dishes into the sink and then cleaning them before putting them into the sanitizing machine gave Willie Jr. plenty of time to think about his life.

What am I going to do next? What about Brenda? What about the church?

Sugar required that the radio in the kitchen be set on a gospel music station. And the radio happened to be stationed just behind Willie Jr. Between his questions, his ideas, and the familiar songs playing through the radio, Willie Jr. couldn't help but have his thoughts mingle with the hymns.

He laughed to himself even now, thinking that this whole scenario sounded like something his father would have set up. Washing dishes was time-consuming, but it didn't take a whole lot of thinking-power. His mind was freed up to imagine what his life would be like if the words of those songs were true—if God really hadn't brought him this far to leave him, if he could have just a closer walk with Jesus, and if only what he did for Christ would last.

If so, Willie Jr. was determined to wash dishes as though he was washing them for the Lord. It was the least he could do after the way he'd dirtied himself with all that stealing and gambling. If he could wash these dishes as clean as He washed Willie, Jr., that was a good thing. A very good thing.

"Willie Jr., go ahead and empty the trash," Rasko, the kitchen manager, ordered.

"Yes, sir."

Rasko had been Sugar's second husband. Their marriage ended amicably, and he still ran the back of the store while Sugar busied herself with the money, the inventory and such.

Willie Jr. brought the dishwashing to a stopping point, removed his apron, and made his way to the men's and women's restrooms. After making sure they were clear, he emptied their trashcans into the bigger bin. Then he got trash from the two receptacles in the low-lit dining area.

"Willie Jr.?" a female voice called. "Is that you?"

He looked at the woman sitting at the table behind him. He barely recognized her. "Anna?"

"Yeah. Anna Dupont. I was a freshman when you were a senior at Pecan Forest High. I had the biggest crush on you!"

"Oh. Hey." Willie smirked. "I would shake your hand, but I'm kind of busy now."

"I see." Anna bugged her eyes. "My word. I've been gone from this town since I graduated. I never thought I would come back home to find *the Willie Lee, Jr.* emptying trashcans at Sugar's. What has the world come to?"

Willie Jr. decided not to take offense. She was obviously a woman scorned; one of the groupies who'd wanted him but he never gave the time of day. And from the looks of that greasy do-rag on her head, he was glad he'd overlooked her. "Live and let live, you know?"

"I guess."

Willie rolled his trash bin to the store's back door. He opened the door, pushing the trash toward the dumpster. The cool night breeze felt good against his skin, especially after experiencing the heat of the kitchen.

Willie Jr. took a breath of fresh air, though it still didn't smell as good as Sugar's ribs.

The trash stopped in its path.

Must be caught on something.

Willie Jr. focused his eyes to determine the problem: A foot. Attached to a leg. Attached to a person. Beaten bloody and barely breathing.

Chapter 15

Galatia paced the floor as she waited on Ephesia to pick her up to take her to Pecan Forest General Hospital. The tone of Willie's voice when he called to tell her that Joseph had been beaten badly scared her. She was sure that whatever happened to Joseph had something to do with Junior's wicked ways.

Ever since the day Galatia requested that Willie be removed as Pastor, she and Joseph had been having their own church services at home. If it had not been for Willie Jr. none of this would be happening. It was his fault that she could no longer come to Lee Chapel. He had embarrassed her and tried to make a fool out of her and her husband.

The blaring of Ephesia's car horn disturbed her thoughts, bringing her back to reality. Galatia grabbed her purse and rushed out the door.

"Hey, I got here as fast as I could," Ephesia said.

"Thank you for coming 'cause I know you could give a rats fat foot if Joseph lives or dies," Galatia pointed out.

"Why would you say that?"

"I'm saying it cause it's the truth. You ain't never cared for Joseph," Galatia added.

"I will admit that he's not my favorite person but I would never wish for something bad like this to happen to him."

"Umm hmm." Galatia rolled her eyes.

Ephesia decided not to respond to Galatia and drove the rest of the way in silence and in prayer for her sister. She knew it would only be a matter of time before Galatia found out who Joseph really is. She wasn't sure how Galatia would react because she placed so much hope in him. Ephesia often wondered if Galatia was pretending or if she was truly blinded by it all.

Ephesia pulled up under the small shed for the emergency room entrance to let Galatia out, and she went to find a parking spot.

Galatia went through the door and walked down the long, dingy hallway. It seemed like the closer she got, the faster her heart beat. By the time she made it to the nurse's station, she was a nervous wreck.

"May I help you?" the nurse asked.

"I'm looking for my husband, Joseph Dewberry," Galatia said almost in a whisper.

The nurse glanced at the computer screen as she tapped on the keyboard. "He's on the third floor in critical care. The elevator is around the corner."

Galatia stood there in a daze. Hearing that Joseph was in critical care placed her in a state of shock.

"Ma'am? Ma'am? Did you hear me?"

The nurse came from around the desk and helped Galatia to the nearest seat, because she looked as if she was going to pass out.

Ephesia was walking up the hallway and rushed

over to assist.

"What's going on? What happened?" she asked.

"Jo-jo-seph is in critical care," Galatia sputtered.

"Don't get yourself all worked up before we speak to the doctor. Don't think the worse," Ephesia offered.

"Ma'am, he's on the third floor, and I believe the doctor is making his rounds now," the nurse said.

"We'll head up there now." Ephesia thanked the nurse and helped Galatia out of the chair.

The two sisters walked hand and hand to the elevator.

Galatia stared at room 3431, unsure if she wanted to go in. She took a few deep breaths and walked in with Ephesia by her side.

Joseph laid in the hospital bed with his head wrapped in badges and tubes down his throat. He was wrapped up so tight that he looked like a mummy. The doctor stood on the opposite side of the bed checking the monitors.

"Oh my God! Joseph, baby, who did this to you?" Galatia sobbed as she approached the side of the bed.

"Are you Mrs. Dewhickey, Joseph's mother?" the doctor inquired.

"She's his wife," Ephesia answered, stroking Galatia's back.

"My apologizes, Mrs. Dewhickey. I'm Dr. Harvey. If I could get you to follow me down to the conference room, I can discuss your husband's condition with you," he said, taking a few steps toward the door.

"Come on, Galatia. Let's follow Dr. Harvey."

Dr. Harvey was a tall, light skinned man who looked to be in his mid-fifties. He exited the room and Galatia and Ephesia followed him to the small conference room.

The conference room consisted of a round table and four chairs. On the far right wall was another table with a coffeemaker, cups, and sugar.

"Would you ladies like a cup of coffee?" he offered.

"I just need to know what happened to my husband, and why is his head bandaged all up?" Galatia blurted out.

"Mr. Dewhickey got beat pretty bad. The trauma to his brain has caused it to swell and his ribs are broken. I have to be honest with you; he's in a coma and right now. Things are touch and go."

"Touch and go...what do you mean by that?" Galatia yelled.

"It means that right now your husband is in God's hands."

"Oh God! Please, Lord, don't take Joseph away from me. I love him so much. He's all I got. Jesus help me. Jesus help me. Lord, Jesus help me, please." Galatia wailed.

"Shhhhhh, it's going to be okay." Ephesia got out of her chair and went to comfort her sister.

"Do you have any children or family members other

than your nephew that you need to contact?" Dr. Harvey asked.

"They don't have any children, and I'm assuming the nephew that you are speaking of is my son. Where is he?" Ephesia inquired.

"He's been down in the chapel ever since Mr. Dewhickey arrived."

"He don't need to be nowhere near Joseph. He's the reason why my husband is here," Galatia spat.

"Galatia, I know you are upset about Joseph's condition but Willie Jr. has nothing to do with this. He was at work and found Joseph in the dumpster so you ought to be thanking and praising God that he found him and got him here."

"Why would they dump him at Willie Jr.'s job? Why there of all the places in the world? It's a sign that Willie Jr. ain't right and he ain't never gon' be right. If right showed up and offered him fifty dollars to do right, he would still take wrong. As a matter of fact, I'm calling the police and telling them to arrest Junior."

"Now I know you done flipped out," Ephesia yelled.

"Ladies, ladies, calm down. This is not the time nor the place to be arguing. Mrs. Dewhickey I'm not a rocket scientist but it's pretty obvious that whoever did this to your husband was planning to kill him. In most cases and from my years of experience, things like this happen from a drug deal gone wrong or if someone owes someone a huge amount of money. The police have already been here to take the report but the truth of the matter is that nothing else can be done. There are no witnesses or at least none willing to come forward and I'm certain that won't happen. Joseph is the only person that knows what happened. Your nephew called the ambulance and rode in the ambulance with your husband. That doesn't sound like someone who wants to harm him. Right now your focus should be praying for God to work a miracle, because your husband is fighting for his life."

"Dr. Harvey is right. Ephesia, we are family and I know right now you are struggling to process this but you really need to be in prayer. We need to contact the church and get Pastor Sanders and the Deacon board to come and pray over him."

"They don't care nothing about us. We been gone from the church and ain't nobody even bothered to find out where we been."

"Galatia, you've only missed three Sundays and I'm sure Pastor Sanders would want to be here. It's time for you to humble yourself and stop trying to fight against the people who really love and care about you. We know that you are one tough cookie. Daddy always said you were strong-willed and bull-headed. You don't always have to be the strong one. You don't have to act like you don't need people. We all need someone, especially during the times when the storms of life are raging. I just lost my husband so I know all kinds of thoughts are running through your head. I know your heart is racing and you're afraid. You don't have to handle this by yourself. Lean on me, lean on the church. That's what we are here for. Let us be your support system," Ephesia pleaded.

Galatia didn't say a word. She simply nodded and dropped her head and cried. Ephesia was right; she'd spent her whole life pretending to have it together, pretending to not care, pretending that she could handle things on her own, when the truth was that she was falling apart.

Chapter 16

Willie Jr. lowered himself at the silent altar in the hospital's chapel. The cushioned knee-bench had been his only companion for these past few hours. The only break had come when he went to the restroom and then got a candy bar from the vending machine to quiet his rumbling stomach.

In his days of playing football, Willie had seen and even heard a lot of injuries occur during practices and on the dangerous playing fields. Broken legs, cracked ribs, and the sound of fellow players screaming in agony while they waited for the team doctors to rush out onto the field were simply a part of the game. Football was definitely a dangerous sport. Everyone who played took a risk, knowing that any play might be their last.

But seeing Joseph's face pounded to a pulp, watching the puddle of crimson blood under his head, and seeing the streams flow from every opening on his face had given Willie Jr. a picture he wished he'd never seen in the first place.

Evidently, gambling was more dangerous than football.

When the images wouldn't leave his brain, Willie Jr. had come down to the chapel to pray and clear his mind. This vision of his uncle clinging to life gave Willie Jr. an even greater respect for those in the

CaSandra McLaughlin & Michelle Stimpson

military. He couldn't imagine having to rescue another comrade in battle under pressure the way he'd rescued Joseph in the back alley.

"God, bless the soldiers," he whispered under his breath. He clasped his hands tighter and squeezed his eyes shut, willing his mind to think of something else.

But Joseph's broken face remained in the mental picture.

And then Willie began to get another vision—his own face trampled to a nearly unrecognizable state. If he hadn't stopped gambling when he did, the people who beat up Joseph probably would have beaten him up, too.

It could have been me. It should have been me. But God. For reasons all His own, He had changed Willie's heart and caused him to turn around before it was too late.

The revelation swept over Willie Jr. like a flood of cleansing water. Every breath he took, every time he walked without a limp, every time he opened his mouth—he owed it all to God. "Thank You, Lord. Thank You," Willie Jr. began to chant. The hospital chapel probably wasn't the usual place for a one-man revival, but he couldn't help it.

All those things the old saints used to sing about— how God picked them up, turned them around, and placed their feet on solid ground—they weren't just old songs anymore. They were *his* testimony now, too. "Lord, I'm sorry I ran. I'm sorry I didn't want to listen.

But I thank You for sending Jesus to die in my place, and I believe on Him and receive Him now as my Savior. For real."

Willie's body trembled as he clapped and cried out to the Lord. *But God.*

He felt like running up the main aisle and turning a cartwheel. He was free! Free from the old man who used to convince Willie Jr. that God's ways were robbing him of all the fun things in life. Obviously, this "fun" led to death in more ways than one—death of relationships, death of self-respect, death itself.

But now, with his life hidden in Christ just the way his father had preached all those years, Willie Jr. could move forward in the things of God.

"Old things are passed away. Hallelujah!" Willie Jr. almost scared himself by the loudness of his voice. He didn't care, though. He'd tell anyone who asked why he was praising God.

And he got that chance right away, as a middle-aged Caucasian woman who must have quietly entered the room as Willie was praising God giggled. She was kneeling at the bench to his right at the altar.

"You must be really glad about something," she said. "Strikes me kind of odd, seeing as we're in a hospital."

"Oh, no." Willie laughed. "This is the best day of my life. I've practically been in church since I was born. But today, the church is born in *me*."

"Wow. You ought to put that in a book or

something," she said with a friendly grin. She looked up at the podium and sighed.

"You okay?" Willie asked.

The woman shook her head. "Not really. I'm just in here to get away from it all."

"Get away from *what* all?" Willie found himself asking, though it wasn't really his nature to prod.

"Sickness. Death. My father's ninety-three. He's lived a good life. My brother and my sister say he's ready to go. And *he* told me he was ready to go, too. But I'm not ready yet. My siblings are twenty years older than me—they had him for much longer than I did."

"Is he a believer?" Willie asked almost instinctively, surprising himself yet again.

"Yes," she admitted with a nod. "I know he's going to a better place."

"Then you'll see him again," Willie assured her, "if you believe as he did."

"Well, I guess I was hoping Jesus would raise my father like he did Lazarus."

Softly Willie answered, "Well, eventually Lazarus did leave again. We all have to go some time or another."

"Why does life have to be so disastrous?" the woman cried, pulling a tissue from her purse and dabbing at her eyes and nose.

"Death isn't a disaster for people who know the Lord," Willie said to her with a wisdom that he could only attribute to the Holy Spirit. He hadn't been saved for-real-for-real for five minutes, and already he was spewing wisdom from a well deep within him.

The woman stood. She smiled at him. "Thank you, young man. I'm going to get back to my dad now and enjoy his final moments. You've been so helpful. Your parents must be proud of you."

Willie's lips turned upward. "Yeah. I think they both are. Now."

A cough interrupted their conversation. Willie turned and looked toward the chapel entrance to see Pastor Grady standing at the entrance.

Slowly, the older man meandered down the aisle. He nodded at the woman as she left the sanctuary. "Good day."

"Yes, it is. Well, I didn't think it was until I talked to that young man." She pointed at Willie Jr. "He's quite the preacher."

"I agree," Grady said.

Willie Jr. quickly wiped the remnants of tears away.

Grady kneeled next to him on the bench. "No need in trying to hide who you are or what you've been through today, Willie Jr. This ain't quite the place or the way where I thought God would make His grand entrance into your life, but His ways are perfect and His thoughts are higher than ours. Welcome to the family of God, son."

Willie Jr. embraced Grady. His only wish at that point was that he had listened to his father sooner than later.

But even now, he was grateful because he truly believed what he'd told the woman. *I will see him again.*

Chapter 17

Galatia sat by Joseph's bedside feeling hopeless. Three days had passed and his condition still hadn't changed. Joseph was still in an induced coma to allow his brain to heal. The doctor and nursing staff told her to go home and get some rest and if anything changed they would call her. Galatia was fearful that if she left, Joseph would pass away. *Lord please, please hear my cry. Don't take him away from me, he didn't mean to let Willie Jr. get him in this mess.*

The slight knock on the door interrupted her.

"Come in," she responded.

Ephesia entered the room with a bag of food from Boston Market.

"I figured since you wouldn't leave to go eat, I'd bring you some food. I brought your favorite—ribs, sweet potato casserole, and creamed spinach" she said as she sat the food on the small table over in the corner and pulled out a chair to sit down.

"I can't eat nothing, but thanks anyway."

"If you don't eat something, you're going to make yourself sick."

"I can't get no sicker than I already am. This whole thing has my stomach in knots, and he ain't getting no better. He just laying there looking lifeless." She sniffed, trying to keep herself from crying.

"Watch your words, Galatia. Speak what you want

to see, not what you think you see. Remember death and life are in the power of the tongue."

"Well, I can't help it, Ephesia. I'm...I'm scared," she blurted out.

"We've all had moments where we may feel fear trying to rise up in us but we must remember that God didn't give us a spirit of fear. The enemy wants to make you have negative thoughts. You have to tell him to flee. Tell him what the word says and trust and believe he will leave you alone."

"It's not that simple, and it's easy for you to say that 'cause it ain't you."

"Galatia, it is that simple when you have God carrying you through it. It's Him that gives us the strength to overcome it all. Remember when Mama use to sing Jesus is on the main line tell Him what you want?"

"I remember her singing that song all day, every day," Galatia said.

"She was right. We can just call Him up and tell Him cause He certainly is listening and He will answer," Ephesia ministered to her sister.

"I don't think He's listening to me 'cause if He was, Joseph would be wide wake."

"His timing isn't our timing. Just be patient."

"Ephesia, why you always gotta give me a sermon when you talking to me?"

"I'm not giving you a sermon. I'm giving you the truth. Giving you some words of encouragement. I

don't understand why you are always so defensive."
Ephesia sighed.

"I'm not defensive. I—" Galatia stopped mid-sentence as a guy dressed in an all black sweat suit with a black beanie on his head entered the room. He was 7'0" and looked as if he weighed every bit of 375 pounds. Galatia and Ephesia exchanged glances. Galatia was sitting close to the bed but not close enough to ring the nurse's station for security.

"Say, ma'am. You Joseph's ole lady?" he asked, sucking his teeth.

"Who-who are you?" Galatia sputtered.

"Just answer the question," he snapped.

Ephesia eyed Galatia letting her know to cool it.

"Yes, I'm his wife. What can I do for you?" she replied.

"You can tell your husband he got 'til tomorrow night to get me my money."

"He can't do that. As you can see, he's not awake. The doctors put him in a coma."

"Well *somebody* better come up with it or else I'll have to pay you a visit over off Hudson. I don't play about my money," he warned.

"How much money did Willie get from you?" Galatia asked.

"I don't know no Willie. Your husband, Jojo, owe me four thousand dollars."

"Sir, will you take a check?" Ephesia asked.

"Do I look like a fool to you?" he spat.

"I'll be back tomorrow. I need my money in cash. No gimmicks. No cops. I know where you live so don't try to play me. You understand?" he said, moving closer to Galatia.

She nodded her head to let him know she understood.

He walked over to the hospital bed, patted Joseph on the chest, and said, "You better hope and pray that I get my money 'cause if I don't, you gon' be dead and your wife will be, too," he said with an evil chuckle and walked out of the room.

"Lord have mercy, Galatia! Now do you see that Joseph ain't no good? Gangsters probably been watching us for days. Ain't no telling what they're capable of doing. We gotta get you out of this mess!" Ephesia exclaimed.

"Joseph wouldn't be involved with somebody like that," Galatia said.

"I can't believe this. You mean to tell me that you're still in denial. What is it going to take to get you to see him for who he really is? A man dressed in black, who knows where you live, has threatened to kill you. This is *real*, Galatia. Why do you insist on being with this man?"

"I love Joseph. He's the only man who has ever paid me some attention. I don't want to lose him."

"Galatia, this man has done nothing but used you up. He's never had a stable job, he drives your car, moved into your house, and runs up all your credit cards. A man who loves you wouldn't do that. Joseph is an opportunist and that's why I didn't want you to marry him. You're worried about losing him but I'm worried about losing you. You're my sister and I won't lose you behind him." Ephesia choked back her tears.

"I just don't know what to do. I don't want to be by myself."

"You have family, so you won't be by yourself, but most importantly you have God. I'm going to go get the money so that we can pay this goon off. You can come and stay with me. I don't want you by yourself."

"What about Joseph?" Galatia cried.

"He's in the Lord's hand. There's nothing you can do for him except pray."

Galatia stood up and hugged her sister. She held on for a while.

"I'm sorry. I'm so sorry I accused Junior for this mess. I knew in my heart that he wouldn't do anything like this. I wanted to believe Joseph, but as usual he lied to me. I've been miserable this whole marriage. I can't do this no more. I can't lie to myself no more. Please forgive me." she sobbed.

"Galatia, I've already forgiven you. It's going to be okay. Come on, let's get out of here."

Ephesia grabbed her purse and headed towards the door. Galatia walked over to Joseph's bedside and starred at him with tears in her eyes. She stood there for about two minutes silently and then followed Ephesia out of the room.

Chapter 18

The moment Joseph's eyes opened, his back ached like nothing he'd ever experienced before. And his face felt like it was being held together only by the stitches and gauze wrapped around his forehead and chin. It probably was, judging by what he had seen in the mirror when he begged he nurse to let him get a look at himself.

"Mr. Dewhickey, you've been in a coma for six days. You're lucky to be alive."

"Wouldn't call this lucky."

"From what I understand, one of your family members—Willie?—found you in an alley."

Joseph peered closer. He barely recognized himself. "I look like a monster."

"Don't get discouraged by the swelling. It will go down in a few weeks," the young nurse had informed Joseph as he studied his reflection in the mirror she held a few feet from him.

He wanted to wince at the sight, but it hurt too much to try to move any muscle in his swollen, stitched-up face.

The only part of his body that didn't hurt was his legs, and that was only because Big Ray had been somewhat merciful. Joseph had a flashback, remembering that one of Big Ray's followers standing over him with a bat, ready to smash Joseph's legs to pieces.

"No!" Big Ray had grabbed the bat. "Don't break his legs and don't mess with his hands. He needs his feet to bring me my money and his hands to count it out. All four thousand dollars."

But apparently he didn't need a head, nose, a jaw, eyes, or a ribcage because they'd been pounded mercilessly.

"Joseph? Baby, you're awake!" Galatia rushed to his side.

The nurse took the mirror away and made room for his wife to sit next to him.

Galatia leaned over him as though she was about to hug him.

"Don't touch me," he managed to declare just in time.

"Oh. I'm sorry." Galatia's brows furrowed in confusion.

"Ma'am, he's quite banged up. Hugging him would be quite painful," the nurse explained.

"Oh." Galatia sighed. "I understand. May I kiss him?"

"Nu uh," Joseph answered. He didn't want to take any risks.

"I'll let the doctor know that he's up," the nurse said as she left the room.

Joseph looked up at his wife's face. He appreciated her being there, but in all honesty, he didn't like the view. Galatia looked even older from the angle of him lying down and her standing over him. She was old when he met her, but now she looked like she could have been his mother.

"Joseph, we need to talk," Galatia started in.

"I can't," he murmured. "Mouth hurts."

"Alright, then, you just listen." She sat down and scooted her chair closer to him. "Joseph, you're a miracle. You should have been dead and gone right now, but God has spared your life. He's given you a second chance. You need to turn your life around and honor him."

He started his spiel, "My life *is* turned around. If I hadn't been hanging around Willie Jr. and the wrong crowd—"

"Joseph, you *are* the wrong crowd! It done took me a long time to see it, but this ain't about Willie Jr., this is about *you!*" she confronted him.

He hadn't been prepared for such a sharp turnaround.

"Now, look, Joseph. Either you stop this lifestyle, or I'm going to have to seek the Lord about whether or not He wants us to stay married." Galatia put her foot down.

"That's easy. God hates divorce." Joseph quoted scripture.

"He also hates lying, stealing, cheating, and wickedness." Galatia summarized a few scriptures of her own.

Joseph studied his wife's stern face. Her expression was set in flint. Far more resolved than he'd ever seen this woman. He wondered who had gotten in his wife's ear. Probably Ephesia and some more ladies from Lee Chapel. "Who have you been talking to?"

"The Lord."

He didn't have a comeback for that one. "Then I guess you gotta do what you gotta do. Don't let me stop you." Joseph looked up at the ceiling again. His head throbbed not only from the physical pain, but from the idea that Galatia might actually be getting some sense in her head—which would be the end of his gravy train.

"Well, in the meantime, you need to figure out how you gonna pay your loan sharks back. I done already borrowed the money from Ephesia to put a down payment on what you owe. That's the only reason that big joker ain't come in here and slit your throat while you was in a coma. But he'll be back. And until you get things in order, I'm stayin' at my sister's house." Galatia rose to her feet.

"Deuces," Joseph said.

Galatia swiveled around. "What?"

He should have known his old lady wouldn't understand. "Never mind. Bye."

Joseph had drifted off to sleep when Galatia left. Whatever medicines they were giving him didn't allow him more than a few hours of consciousness at a time.

He was grateful because the pain in his body was enough to make him slap the judge.

Sometime in the night, he heard the door open but couldn't turn over to see who was coming into the room. Whether it was the doctor or another nurse, he didn't care. He slept soundly.

But the next morning, he saw the note taped to the rail on his bed: *Paye Up or Dy.* Had to be Big Ray himself, spelling like that.

Joseph snatched the note off the rail and balled it in his fist. The thought that his enemy had been in his room and been close enough to kill him made Joseph shudder. He didn't have the money to pay Big Ray now, and probably wouldn't have it ever. He needed to get out of town. Quickly.

The room door creaked open again. This time, Joseph fought the pain to turn and look at the door. If he was going to die, he might as well face his own killer.

Thankfully, the man who entered was Willie Jr. Joseph breathed easier now.

"Hey." Willie Jr. shoved his hands into his pockets awkwardly.

"Hey. Thanks for saving my life."

"No problem," Willie Jr. said. "How do you feel?"

"Like a seven-foot beast sat on my skull," Joseph said. "But I can't worry about that right now." He handed Willie Jr. the note.

Willie Jr. tried to read it. "Pa-yee? Dee?"

Joseph translated, "It says pay up or die."

"Oh. Who—"

"You don't need to know. In fact, the less you know the better, Willie Jr. You were never cut out for this kind of work." Joseph hoisted himself into an upright position. Every breath created a cutting sensation in his chest, but he couldn't focus on that now.

"Dude, you shouldn't be moving—"

"I have to get out of here. And I need your help." Joseph swung his legs off the edge of the bed. Steadied himself before standing. The blood rushed to his head, making him plop back down on the mattress.

"Joseph, you can't leave in this condition. You just got out of a coma," Willie Jr. warned him.

"Well, if I stay in here much longer, I'm going to be six feet under. The man who wrote that note has already been here to threaten me. He'll be back. I can't let him find me here."

Willie Jr. rattled off, "Can't we just get security?"

Joseph hurt himself laughing. "Man, you don't call in the law when you dealin' with lawless folks." He caught his breath.

The whites of his nephew's eyes showed complete shock and utter fear. "Nephew, I never should have gotten you involved in my hustle. I could have gotten you killed. You wasn't cut out for this. Best thing you can do is exactly what your daddy said—be a preacher. You too good for this kind of life. Too scary, too."

Joseph held his arm out as Willie Jr. propped him

up to a standing position. Though Joseph felt dizzy, he didn't collapse this time. "That's good." He took a small step. Another step.

"Where are you going?" Willie Jr. asked.

"Well, where you're taking me is about forty-five minutes out of town. I got family over in Crookshaw County. Word'll get around that I'm gone. The one I owe will come looking for me. Me and my folks will take care of it."

Joseph untapped his wrist and gently pulled the IV out.

"You can't just leave. You haven't been discharged," Willie Jr. fussed.

"Don't you understand? I'm discharging myself," Joseph said as he held the vessel closed long enough stop himself from bleeding to death. He shuffled over to the closet and grabbed a robe.

"Tell Galatia to get everything valuable out of the house and stay put at Ephesia's for now. Once I get with my uncles, we'll figure out a way to handle things. One way or another."

Willie Jr. played look-out for Joseph one last time as they snuck out of the hospital.

Epilogue

Three months later

Willie's Jr.'s feet bounced and his knees shook as he waited for Grady to call him to the side podium. This was perhaps the second most important day of his life, next to the day he realized that his father's prophetic words had come to pass. He really was a minister deep down inside. Maybe not the kind who would lay hands on people's heads and watch them fall down in the Spirit or the kind who wore several titles and aspired to lead a mega-church. In fact, Willie Jr. quietly hoped that Lee Chapel would never become a huge congregation. Even if major companies brought jobs, a Wal-Mart got built in the center of town, and the town of Pecan Forest suddenly became a bubbling suburb like some of the smaller cities they'd play when they were in high school, Willie Jr. still wanted Lee Chapel to have a personal feel.

Or maybe he was just scared to lead.

No matter what, though, he was determined to do his best with whatever the Lord had in store for him. Including this night. Wednesday night Bible study. Grady had asked Willie Jr. to have words at the end of the study, then close them out in prayer.

And Willie Jr. had agreed, but he hadn't anticipated the stirring of anxiety in his chest that consumed him all day. He had read the assigned scriptures—Ephesians 4:1-16, about unity and maturity in the body of Christ. If anyone needed maturity in the body of Christ, Willie Jr. knew he was the one.

Willie Jr. held his breath after Grady finished the offering. *What can I say? What am I going to tell these people who have probably been studying the Bible longer than I have been alive?* The only good thing about starting his "ministry" on a Wednesday night was that only the faithful came to that service. The ones who had been praying for him throughout this whole ordeal. Couldn't have been more than twenty of them in attendance. But Willie Jr. didn't want to turn around and count them all because if there were more than twenty, he'd just be all the more nervous.

The congregants were zipping their Bibles and jingling their keys.

"Church, I know we've all turned our minds toward home, but I would like to ask Willie Jr. to share what's on his heart regarding tonight's lesson. And he'll give the benediction when he's finished."

Willie's chest pounded. His throat tightened. He scooted to the end of his pew and grabbed the back of the pew in front of him.

He got a glimpse of his mother's face. She nodded and smiled.

Beside her was his Aunt Galatia. Surprisingly, she, too, gave Willie Jr. that same nod of reassurance. In fact, Galatia started clapping. Next thing Willie Jr.

knew, everyone was clapping.

Willie Jr. rose to his feet, marveling at the love and support of these people who had been so faithful to his father, to Lee Chapel, and to the Lord himself. His heart seemed to fall to the floor with the weight of humility.

"Come on up, Willie Jr.," Grady prodded.

With the love and support of his natural and spiritual family, Willie walked up to the side podium—reserved for amateurs like himself—and opened his Bible.

His body thumped with emotion. *Am I about to start crying?*

Willie Jr. cleared his throat. Blinked real fast. *I can't go out like that on my first mini-sermon.*

But then, as he looked out on the congregation, he saw something that immediately wrenched every bit of emotion from his chest.

Brenda.

He fixed his eyes on her momentarily. A tear escaped his control. Willie Jr. quickly wiped it away as he grabbed the microphone from Grady.

"Here you go, son."

"Thank you."

"Got something else for you, too," Grady said with a smile.

He put a hand on Willie Jr.'s shoulder. Then he presented Willie Jr. with Willie Sr.'s Bible. "I think you'll be needing this now."

Willie Jr. couldn't contain himself any more. He hugged Grady tightly as the church exploded in a round of applause for Willie Jr. and praise to God.

Ephesia cried out, "Thank You, Lord! Thank You!" Her voice sounded more like wailing, as though a million prayers for her son were being answered in that one moment.

Instantly, Willie Jr. remembered all the times his parents had prayed for him. He remembered the countless times he had seen his father travailing in prayer for loved ones, no doubt including his own son.

The God they had prayed to had protected Willie Jr. from the same fate as Joseph, who was in jail awaiting trial following a deadly shoot-out with Big Ray. Once again, it could have been Willie Jr. in Joseph's shoes, sitting in a jail cell, getting served with divorce papers, and looking at decades of imprisonment.

Instead, here Willie Jr. was. Standing before the church. No criminal record. No side chick. All his teeth in place. His family behind him, and his wife there to support him...maybe.

Thank You, Jesus.

Willie opened his father's Bible to Ephesians chapter 4. Quickly, he read his father's notes in the margins as the church members' applause died down.

"Thanks, everyone," Willie Jr. said. "I appreciate your support more than you know." He sniffed. Composed himself. "We had a great lesson tonight already. There's not much more I can add. But I did want to say something that's kind of funny."

The congregation chuckled even before he could say what was funny. "I owe you all the biggest apology. I know some of you have heard rumors. I know some of you have seen me do things you thought were questionable. And I'm here to tell you tonight that it was all true. Whatever you heard, it was probably worse. And I'm sorry. I repent to the Lord. To this church. To my mother. And to my wife."

Willie pointed at Brenda, who was dabbing her eyes with a tissue.

"But this note I just saw in my father's Bible is perfect for this moment. Like God knew everything would work out just the way it has. The fourth chapter of Ephesians, verses eleven through fourteen reads, 'And he gave some, apostles; and some, prophets; and some, evangelists; and some, pastors and teachers; For the perfecting of the saints, for the work of the ministry, for the edifying of the body of Christ: Till we all come in the unity of the faith, and of the knowledge of the Son of God, unto a perfect man, unto the measure of the stature of the fullness of Christ: That we henceforth be no more children, tossed to and fro, and carried about with every wind of doctrine, by the sleight of men, and cunning craftiness, whereby they lie in wait to deceive.'"

The power of the Word seemed to seep into Willie Jr.'s bones. "And my father's note in the margin says, 'Lord, make Willie Jr. strong. Plant him in you. Keep him from crafty deception. Preserve him for Your service.'"

The members moaned with the same realization.

"I think," Willie said, "no, I know that God has a plan for each of us. Whatever gift He has given us, we need to use it for His glory. Because in the end, it's not going to be about money or fame or fortune, but what we did with the risen Christ. Did we believe on Him? And...that's all I can think of right now because I'm still overwhelmed with everything."

Lee Chapel gave him a supportive laugh.

"Let the Lord use you!" Aunt Galatia blurted out.

"Yes, ma'am," Willie Jr. respectfully answered, to which they all laughed again.

He took a deep breath. "I just want to thank you all for praying for me. For not giving up on me." He looked at Brenda again. "With the help of the Lord, I will do my best to serve Him and you faithfully, fully, and reverently."

Brenda gave a slight nod. The twinkle of hope in her eyes said it all. She would give him one more chance. And that was all Willie Jr. needed because this time, he was leaning on the Lord to help him become the man everyone who loved him dearly had obviously already seen.

Now, it was time to shine in His glory.

Enjoy this author duo?
You'll love their Blended Blessings Series!
Here's a Sneak Peek at Book 1: *A New Beginning*

Description: Sometimes love doesn't work out the first time. Or the second. Now in her third marriage, Angelia is hoping for her happily-ever-after with former pro-football player Darren Holley. But soon after they move into their sprawling mini-mansion, Darren's new job as a high school football coach in a trophy-hungry Texas town consumes him, leaving Angelia feeling like a single mother to her two children as well as Darren's twin diva-daughters. Not to mention the drama from Darren's mother, who can't get over the fact that her son has married a woman with so much baggage.

When Angelia confides in a few ladies from the local church, their nice, sweet, holy-wife advice may prove ineffective and too burdensome. Should Angelia cut her losses and get out before the ink settles on their marriage certificate, or will she finally learn the true meaning of marriage as she and Darren attempt to blend two very different backgrounds in the face of adversity *and* nosy church folk?

A New Beginning is the first book in the Blended Blessings series by newcomer CaSandra McLaughin and bestselling author Michelle Stimpson.

* * *

Chapter 1

I closed my eyes and opened them again to make sure I wasn't dreaming. I wanted to be sure that this beautiful 2-story, 6-bedroom, 3 full bath, 2 half-bath house was really mine. Darren had told me that he was ready for us to get settled in a house, but never in a million years did I think it would be like this. I'd seen gated communities on TV and even joked with Darren about living next door to Tyler Perry or even owning a home similar to T.I. and Tiny's. I never expected Lancing Springs, Texas to have houses this beautiful.

"Angelia, do you like it?"

"Oh my God, Darren, are you kidding me? I love it, honey and I love you too." I ran into his arms and planted a big kiss on his lips. "I can't wait to decorate every room."

"Come on, baby let's get unpacked; we can worry about decorating later. Amber, Marcus, come on, let's get these boxes in the house."

I stood there watching Darren unload the U-Haul truck. I took out my cell phone and decided to take a few selfies with our new house in the background. I couldn't wait to for all of my family and friends to see that I was *finally* getting it right. After two failed marriages, I *finally* understood that the good guy really is the best choice.

The first time around, I was married to my daughter Amber's dad, Javar Norell. Javar and I were only together for three years. I honestly thought that we would be together forever, that is, until he started drinking. Javar was a very spontaneous guy. He loved to hang out, take road trips and loved spoiling me with gifts, but I never knew how he was able to afford those gifts. I was so far gone that if Javar told me to jump, I asked how high. My mind was just gone, but that's what happens when you're young and in love.

Javar worked for a pest control company for a living, but after being with him for about a year I heard rumors pertaining to him selling drugs. Turns out, those "road trips" we were taking were actually drug deals.

One night Javar and his brother, Leo were at a party and the police raided the place. Javar got into a shootout with officers. He severely injured one cop and was shot by another. He survived the gunshot wound, but he might as well have been dead to me, because he's serving a life sentence without a chance for parole.

Witnesses said that Javar was about to surrender when the police started shooting at him. I was devastated and wanted some answers from the police but wasn't successful in getting them. When I gave birth to Amber several months later, I filed for divorce and moved on with my life.

That was seventeen years ago. Amber's a college-bound senior. She's the quiet, nervous type and she's a loner and that's probably because she was the only child for such a long time. Needless to say she's never given me any trouble and she helps me out a lot with Demarcus.

After Javar came Marcus or should I say *Mr. America*. Marcus is good looking, a Tyrese look alike and he knows it. I've never in my life met a man who stayed in the mirror more than me. Marcus was a great provider and he fulfilled all my needs—and the needs of every other woman he met too. The funny thing about Marcus is that I would catch him cheating and he would lie and sweet talk me into staying with him. The final straw for me was when I found out he had a baby on the way. There I was all in la la land in love with him and so was Trisha; we were pregnant at the same time. Our children were born two days apart. My son Demarcus is eight years old now.

I made up my mind that I was done with love. I had planned to raise my children and be by myself until I met Darren. I remember going to Wal-Mart on an ice cream run. I absolutely love pecan pralines and cream ice cream and was having a serious craving. I threw on some sweats, a t-shirt and my baseball cap and went to the store. I went straight to the ice cream aisle and was livid when I realized they were out of my favorite ice cream. I guess Darren noticed the disgusted look on my face and it prompted him to come see what was going on.

"Is there something I can help you with? You seem to be upset?"

"Well unless you work for Bluebell, ain't a thing you can do for me."

I was truly irritated by him.

"Well you might be in luck." Darren reached in his basket and gave me his ice cream, my favorite, pecan pralines and cream.

I stood there with a huge smile on my face and I thanked him. He asked me for my number. At first I was a little hesitant but then thought, *Sure...why not.* Darren called me that night and we talked for hours. We even slept on the phone. I was so taken by him, I loved how we were able to share so much in just one night.

He told me about his previous marriage and about his twin daughters, Tyler and Skylar. Darren explained to me that he played professional football for two years but had to quit following a terrible knee injury. His ex-wife, Marcy was all for their marriage until he got hurt. Marcy started straying away from him and things around the house became tense. Darren is a family man so he tried to stay for the sake of his girls, but eventually the stress of being unhappy became too much for him to bear.

"I'm not going to lie," he admitted, "I could have been a better husband. But we were both in it for the wrong reasons to begin with, I think. Just young and stupid."

Of course, I could relate.

Darren and Marcy divorced and she and the girls moved to Lancing Springs. Darren threw himself into working as a supervisor at UPS. It wasn't the dream job but it's what paid the bills while he earned a teaching certificate and coached league football on the side. Because he'd made wise investments with his NFL earnings, he was still in good shape financially. So while he knew that teaching wasn't the highest-paying career, the ongoing dividends from short and long-term investments would always provide a comfortable lifestyle.

Darren and I started dating and fell in love real quick.

I wasn't used to having a good man, so I had to learn to adjust. Darren is truly one of a kind so when he asked me to be his wife, there was no doubt in my mind that he was the one. Darren loves the game of football. Football is his life, which is why we're here in Lancing Springs. One of Darren's coaching friends told him about an opening for the assistant coach position here at the high school. Darren interviewed for the job and here we are. Although Lancing Springs is different from my hometown, Dallas, Texas, I'm sure I'll adjust. I can always go home to visit; it's only an hour away.

"Baby, what are you doing?" Darren interrupted my thoughts.

"I'm just admiring the house, still can't believe it's ours."

"Well believe it." He pulled me close and hugged me tight. "Mrs. Holley, I love you."

"I love you too, Mr. Holley. Or should I say *Coach* Holley?"

"Coach Holley. Babe, you don't know how good it feels to be here. This is a dream come true. I'm finally getting my chance to be a coach."

"Honey, you deserve it. You're going to help take this team to the playoffs."

"Babe, thanks for believing in me and standing by my side. Let's do a little more unpacking and then we'll grab a bite to eat."

"Okay, sounds good; I'll go upstairs and check on the kids." Darren kissed me again and to my surprise, swatted my behind.

Demarcus cried, "Ewwww!" from the top of the staircase. He ran out of sight.

"You shouldn't have been spying!" I teased my son, though I was quite glad that he could now witness healthy affection between a man and a woman. I hoped that someday he would love his wife as much as I believed Darren loved me.

I was enjoying our moment until the phone rang.

"Baby, I'll get the phone, you go check on the kids."

"Hello," I practically sang into the phone.

"Hey Angelia, sweetheart, how are you?"

"I'm fine, Mother Holley we're trying to get settled in."

153

Vivian Holley is my mother-in-law. She is trying to get used to the fact that I stole her baby boy's heart and she also has an issue with this being my third marriage. When Darren and I married I started out calling her mom, but she insisted that I call her Mother Holley.

"Okay dear, I was just checking in with you all. I'm so happy for y'all; God is doing some great things for you and Darren so hopefully you can find a church for your family to join."

I try my best to tune Mother Holley out; every time I talk to her she shoves the church down my throat. Mother goes to church every other day and is involved in every ministry they have, from the Usher board to the Sunshine committee. I grew up in church but that wasn't my thing.

"Angelia, I think it's a great start and exactly what you need so when Darren gets custody of the girls you'll all be one big happy saved family."

"Custody of the girls!" I yelled before I knew it. My head was about to explode.

"Yes dear, that's part of the reason why Darren accepted the job, so that he can get custody of Tyler and Skylar."

I felt my blood boiling.

"Angelia, surely you didn't think that you moved into a house that huge just for your kids," Mother Holley said with an evil chuckle.

I was starting to sweat and needed to get off the phone with her before I said something I couldn't take back.

"Angelia, are you still there, dear? Didn't Darren talk to you about his plans?"

I could just wring this woman's neck; she knew good and well that I was clueless about this. I took a few deep breaths and replied,

"Umm … yes, we discussed it, but the decision isn't final as of yet. Mother Holley, I've got to go. Thanks for checking on us."

I hung up the phone before she could respond. *How could Darren keep something this important from me? Those girls can't move in and tear up my house.* Don't get me wrong, I like Tyler and Skylar, but living with them simply will not work. Skylar and Tyler are cut from a different cloth. I wouldn't call them ghetto, but they are a little unruly—but that's not *their* fault. Children do what they see, so in their case the apple don't fall far from the tree. It seems like every time Darren gets a call from Marcy, it's always about the twins fighting or getting expelled from school.

I'm so glad that my baby girl, Amber is nothing like those two. Amber is a straight-A student and wants to become an attorney. After learning about her father's questionable incarceration, Amber decided she wanted to be an attorney. She watches every TV show pertaining to law, especially after the Michael Brown and Eric Garner cases. Amber loves to read and she's never had a boyfriend. I'm hoping the move here will help her come out of her shell and I don't need those girls ruining my plans.

"Babe, Demarcus has his clothes unpacked and Amber's moping around, not really sure what's going on with her. Babe, did you hear me?"

"Oh honey, I'm sorry. I heard you, I was just deep in thought."

"Who was that on the phone?"

"Oh that was your mother calling to check on us. Let me go check on Amber so that we can go."

I climbed the stairs still heated about my conversation with Mother Holley. I had to find a way to ask Darren about the twins but not today. I wanted to enjoy my family and my beautiful house. I knocked on Amber's door but there was no answer. I entered the room and she was lying on the bed with her headphones on.

"Amber … baby girl, why haven't you unpacked your clothes?"

"Mom, I don't know. I'll get around to it."

"What's wrong?"

"I was feeling a little hot earlier and nauseous."

"It's probably from the excitement of the move and maybe even a little anxiety. You probably just need to eat something; come on, let's go. Darren wants to take us out to eat.

"Mom, can you just bring me something back? I really just want to stay here."

"Okay baby, are you sure? Maybe we should take you to the doctor."

"No Mom, I don't need a doctor; you're probably right, it's the excitement of the move. I'll be fine. I'll shower and take a nap and when you guys return I'll be all better."

"Well okay, Amber, if you say so; call me on my cell phone if you need to."

"Okay Mom, I will." I kissed her cheek and left the room. Something didn't seem right. Maybe she was just nervous about the move. *Yeah, I'm sure that's all it is; otherwise, she'd tell me if there was a problem. Wouldn't she?*

A New Beginning
Available in Print & Ebook Format Now!

About the Authors

CaSandra McLaughlin was raised in Marshall, Texas. Growing up she wrote poems and loved to read books. She remembers being excited every time the book mobile came to her school. Reading always took her to another place, and often she would find herself rewriting an author's story. CaSandra wrote a play in high school for theatre that she received a superior rating on, and from there she aspired to be a writer.

CaSandra's a true believer that God has blessed us all with gifts and talents and it's up to us to tap into them to make our dreams come true. She's always dreamed of being on radio, TV and being an author. CaSandra currently works for a Gospel radio station and now she's an author. That lets her know that dreams come true—two down and one more to go. CaSandra wants people to read her work and feel encouraged, and it's her prayer that they read something that will change their lives and give them a ray of hope that things will be better. She's praying that God will continue to use her to write novels with several life lessons to help inspire the world.

CaSandra currently lives in Glenn Heights, Texas with her husband Richard and they have two amazing children. CaSandra loves God, her family, church, her friends, reading and Mexican food, in that order. Peace and blessings to all. Thanks for the love and support. Visit CaSandra McLaughlin Online at
www.CaSandraMcLaughlin.com
http://www.facebook.com/casandra.marshallmclaughlin

Michelle Stimpson's works include the highly acclaimed *Boaz Brown, Divas of Damascus Road* (National Bestseller), and *Falling Into Grace,* which has been optioned for a movie. She has published several short stories for high school students through her educational publishing company at WeGottaRead.com. Michelle serves in women's ministry at her home church, Oak Cliff Bible Fellowship. She regularly speaks at special events and writing workshops sponsored by churches, schools, book clubs, and educational organizations.

The Stimpsons are proud parents of two young adults—one in college, one serving in the military—and one crazy dog.

Visit Michelle online:
www.MichelleStimpson.com
https://www.facebook.com/MichelleStimpsonWrites

Other Books by CaSandra McLaughlin

A New Beginning (Book 1 in the Blended Blessings
Series with Michelle Stimpson)
Through It All (Book 2 in the Blended Blessings Series
with Michelle Stimpson)
Peace of Mind (Book 3 in the Blended Blessings Series
with Michelle Stimpson)
Redemption

Other Works by Michelle Stimpson

Fiction

A Forgotten Love (Novella) Book One in the "A Few
Good Men" Series
The Start of a Good Thing (Novella) Book Two in the
"A Few Good Men" Series
A Change of Heart (Novella) Book Three in the "A
Few Good Men" Series
A Shoulda Woulda Christmas (Novella)
Boaz Brown (Book 1 in the Boaz Brown Series)
No Weapon Formed (Book 2 in the Boaz Brown
Series)
Divas of Damascus Road
Falling into Grace
I Met Him in the Ladies' Room (Novella)
Last Temptation (Starring "Peaches" from Boaz
Brown)
Mama B: A Time to Speak (Book 1)
Mama B: A Time to Dance (Book 2)
Mama B: A Time to Love (Book 3)
Mama B: A Time to Mend (Book 4)

Mama B: A Time for War (Book 5)
Mama B: A Time to Plant (Book 6)
Posted
Someone to Watch Over Me
Stepping Down
Stuck on You (Book 1 in the Stoneworths Series)
The Good Stuff
Trouble In My Way (Young Adult)
What About Momma's House? (Novella with April Barker)
What About Love? (Novella with April Barker)
What About Tomorrow? (Novella with April Barker)

Non-Fiction
Did I Marry the Wrong Guy? And other silent ponderings of a fairly normal Christian wife
Leaving the Classroom
Uncommon Sense: 30 Truths to Radically Renew Your Mind in Christ
Speak to Your Food
The 21-Day Publishing Plan

If you like this book, you'll want to read our literary friends!
www.BlackChristianReads.com

CPSIA information can be obtained
at www.ICGtesting.com
Printed in the USA
LVOW08s1726251016

510212LV00002B/349/P

9 781532 862861